"I'm trying to help you! Can't you just accept it?"

"No! Not help from you, anyway! Your family hates mine, Jericho."

When she used his name, Jericho's chest tightened and his nerves sprang to life. Never before had his name sounded so intimate. So personal. So sensual.

"I won't be run out of town."

"I'm not running you out of town."

"Right! What other reason could you possibly have for wanting me to go?"

Knowing she wouldn't believe him if he put this into words, and officially at his frustration limit, Jericho grabbed her shoulders, yanked her to him and kissed her. He kissed her deeply, instantly falling into the act as if he were made to kiss her. He devoured her mouth, tasting her, enjoying her—and she responded. As if she were made to kiss him.

Dear Reader,

This month seems to be all about change. Just as our heroines are about to have some fabulous makeovers, Silhouette Romance will be undergoing some changes over the next months that we believe will make this classic line even more relevant to your challenging lives. Of course, you'll still find some of your favorite SR authors and favorite themes, but look for some new names, more international settings and even more emotional reads.

Over the next few months the company is also focusing attention on the new direction and package for Harlequin Romance. We believe that the blend of authors and stories coming in that line will thrill readers and satisfy every emotion.

Just like our heroines, my responsibilities will be changing, as I will be working on Harlequin NEXT. Please know how much I have enjoyed sharing these heartwarming, aspirational reads with you.

With all best wishes,

Ann Leslie Tuttle
Associate Senior Editor

Please address questions and book requests to:
Silhouette Reader Service
U.S.: 3010 Walden Ave., P.O. Box 1325, Buffalo, NY 14269
Canadian: P.O. Box 609, Fort Erie, Ont. L2A 5X3

With This Kiss

SUSAN MEIER

SILHOUETTE *Romance*®

Published by Silhouette Books

America's Publisher of Contemporary Romance

To the senior editors for Silhouette Romance
who have given us love, laughter and
romance for over two decades.

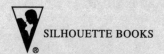 SILHOUETTE BOOKS

ISBN-13: 978-0-373-19827-6
ISBN-10:   0-373-19827-2

WITH THIS KISS

Copyright © 2006 by Linda Susan Meier

This edition published by arrangement with Harlequin Books S.A.

Visit Silhouette Books at www.eHarlequin.com

Printed in U.S.A.

SUSAN MEIER

is one of eleven children, and though she's yet to write a book about a big family, many of her books explore the dynamics of "unusual" family situations, such as large work "families," bosses who behave like overprotective fathers or "sister" bonds created between friends. Because she has more than twenty nieces and nephews, children also are always popping up in her stories. Many of the funny scenes in her books are based on experiences raising her own children or interacting with her nieces and nephews.

She was born and raised in western Pennsylvania and continues to live in Pennsylvania.

Dear Reader,

Every once in a while a story comes along that just tickles a writer's fancy, and *With This Kiss* was that kind of story for me. I love a good makeover. What woman doesn't want to be transformed from average to goddess? But in Rayne Fegan's case the transformation was more fun than normal when she changes from frumpy newspaper reporter to a femme fatale absolutely determined to get her man.

But Jericho Capriotti is in a web of his own making. Years before he'd seen her all decked out at a party and he's been weaving fantasies for years.

The only problem is their families hate each other. It's a Romeo and Juliet with a sexy twist.

I hope you enjoy this final installment in THE CUPID CAMPAIGN!

Susan Meier

Chapter One

When Rayne Fegan stepped inside the Calhoun Corners' borough building, the room instantly quieted. The police officers who sat at two of the four metal desks stopped writing. The two who stood by the blind-covered windows, pouring coffee from the pot perched on the wide ledge, openly stared at her.

No one asked her what she wanted. No one said, "Can I help you?" Everybody just stared.

She strode down the aisle created by the gray metal desks, directly to the office of the chief of police, Jericho Capriotti. Though she honestly believed she would rather be shot than knock on his closed door, she lifted her hand and rapped twice.

"Come in!" he growled.

Rayne ran her fingers along the back of her head to assure that her ponytail was secure, shoved her big glasses up her nose, and took a fortifying breath that she let out slowly before she twisted the knob and walked in.

Jericho sat with his back to the door, signing what looked to be a stack of checks on the credenza behind him. "What's so important that you had to interrupt me?"

"I n-n-need your help," Rayne said, and nearly cursed because she had stuttered with fear. She couldn't believe she was afraid of this man, then decided that technically she wasn't "afraid" as much as she felt as if she were facing judgment day. Jericho Capriotti's dad was mayor of Calhoun Corners. In the last election Rayne and her newspaper editor father had done everything within the bounds of journalistic propriety to unseat him. They never crossed the line. They only printed the truth. But in the op-ed pages of the *Calhoun Corners Chronicle,* where her dad could ask the readers to weigh the facts and carefully consider their choices, Rayne's father had most certainly made it clear that the fourth estate thought it was time for new leadership.

She had tried her best to get Jericho's dad out of office and now when her dad was in trouble, the only person she could turn to was a man who hated her.

"M-m-my dad is missing."

Jericho turned slowly and caught her gaze with his steady green eyes. Wearing a taupe uniform exactly like the officers in the main room out front, he looked formidable and official. But with his brown hair falling to his forehead and his light-colored eyes gleaming with fire, he also looked so darned sexy that Rayne did curse—albeit in her head. All her life she'd been dogged by a crush on this man who was so much older than she was that he'd never given her the time of day. Was it any wonder she'd agreed with her dad that it was time for Capriotti rule of Calhoun Corners to end?

He smiled. "What did you say?"

"You don't have to be so damned happy about the fact that my dad is missing! To me it isn't funny. And you're no longer some sophomoric idiot who's allowed to tease his way through life. You're the chief of police!"

Damn him! Damn them all!

"You're right," Jericho said, then wiped his hand across his face as if forcing himself to get rid of his smile. "I was out of line."

He gestured to an empty chair in front of his desk. "Sit. Can I get you some coffee or tea or something?"

She didn't bother wondering why he hadn't asked her about coming directly to him, instead of simply approaching one of the officers out front. With the feud between their families, she had bypassed his staff and brought the matter to him to assure that he couldn't sidestep responsibility. He had to take the case to prove he wouldn't.

"No coffee. No tea. No anything. I just want help finding my dad."

"Okay."

She primly took the seat he offered, then flipped through her father's small pocket notebook until she found the page she wanted.

She handed the pad across the desk. "As you can see from the date on his note, my dad left almost two weeks ago, but it took me until yesterday to track down and pay off the people he's running from."

Jericho quickly scanned the missive. He didn't even blink when he came to the part where her father admitted he'd been working to unseat Ben Capriotti as a way to pay back the money he'd borrowed from a loan shark. Jericho read impassively, then glanced up at her.

"Rayne, according to this, your dad's not missing."

"Of course he is! He hasn't been home in nearly two weeks."

"But he left a note."

"Which doesn't tell me where he is." Rayne paused, sighed, and decided she needed to start this story from the beginning so he would understand. "I woke up about two weeks ago and found that note on the kitchen table. I immediately began looking for the loan shark," she said, pointing to the name of the man her dad had written. "When I found him I told him I could pay off my dad's debt, but it would take a day or two to get the money together."

"Why did your dad borrow forty thousand dollars?"

Rayne licked her suddenly dry lips. "He wanted to become a breeder."

Jericho leaned back. "Oh."

"Yes!" she all but spat. "And he probably would have made a fortune like your father and brother-in-law, except, as always, my dad isn't lucky."

"Are you insinuating my father is only successful because he's lucky?"

"I have no idea why your dad is successful, but at least his first mare didn't die giving birth."

"What happen to the colt?"

She swallowed. "It died, too."

Jericho put his forearms on the stack of papers on his desk and leaned toward her. "So, he borrowed money for an investment that didn't pan out and couldn't pay it back."

Grateful for the surprisingly kind way he phrased that, Rayne nodded.

"And you paid it back?"

She nodded again. "I had savings." For the past year, she had lived with her dad and hadn't spent money on clothes or entertainment, so she had plenty of cash to save. Now, she wished her dad had let her pay her share of their household expenses. Now, she wished she'd chosen a better outfit than worn jeans and an oversize T-shirt when forced to enter the enemy camp. Now, she wished her dad had simply confided that he wanted the chance to prove himself. She would have *given* him the money to purchase a mare if he had asked.

"So my dad can come home but I can't find him. I don't have the resources. You do."

Jericho shook his head. "Not necessarily. If somebody doesn't want to be found, there are lots of ways they can remain lost for a long time."

Rayne blinked back tears at the very real possibility that she might never see her dad again. "But there's no reason for him to stay away."

Jericho gently said, "He doesn't know that."

Rayne's lip quivered. After meeting the incredibly frightening man from whom her father had borrowed his money, Rayne knew that if her dad believed he still owed that man money, he would stay away forever.

"I do have a suggestion though."

She shot her gaze to Jericho's.

"I know a guy in Vegas who's a skip tracer."

"One of the people who finds defendants who don't show up for trial?"

"Yes, he's up on all the latest technology. He knows

things and can do things the rest of us don't and can't." He caught her gaze. "Do you understand what I'm saying?"

She nodded. A skip tracer could skirt the edges of the law to find someone. A police officer couldn't.

"Do you want his name?"

She nodded again. Jericho wrote a name and telephone number on a piece of paper and handed it to her.

"Here. Tell Mac that I recommended you hire him."

Rising from her seat, Rayne quietly said, "Thanks."

Jericho cleared his throat. "You're welcome."

Rayne left his office. Though her eyes stung with unshed tears, she walked to the door with her head held high. She opened it and marched out and down the street as if absolutely nothing were wrong. But when she entered the empty offices for the *Calhoun Corners Chronicle,* she deflated with misery.

But, just as quickly, she forced herself to stand tall again. She wasn't a quitter and she had the name of a skip tracer, somebody Jericho Capriotti recommended to search for her dad. She would find her dad. She had to.

After Rayne left, Jericho pushed back his squeaky wooden chair, rose and walked into the main room of the police station. Aaron Jennings and Bill Freedman were gone. At seven sharp, they would have jumped into a cruiser to make an early morning sweep of the town, including stops at the elementary, middle and high schools. Greg Hatfield and Martha Wissinger sat at their desks. Martha, a veteran with twenty years on the force and hair she dyed platinum-blond, read the paper. Greg, a twenty-year-old newbie with brown hair who worked out so much his biceps strained against his uniform sleeve, was filling out the report for an incident from the night before. In another twenty minutes, Greg and Martha would go home to get some sleep and spend time with their families before their next shift that evening.

Jericho was in a good town, working with good people. He'd come back to his hometown a reformed man. A respected law enforcement officer. Somebody his parents could be proud of. So why the hell had his brain picked today get a flash of memory of his stupid fantasy about Rayne Fegan?

Jericho didn't want to be even *thinking* any kind of good thought about the daughter of the man who had been a thorn in his family's side for as long as Jericho could remember. He was home. Fences had been mended. His brother Rick was getting married in February. His sister Tia would be a mother in January. And he had a place at the table again for Thanksgiving next week. Only a fool would disturb the family harmony.

Shaking his head, he walked to the window ledge housing the coffeepot. It was insane to scold himself for ideas he had no intention of following through on. Though he could have happily followed through on them three years ago when he'd run into Rayne at a party in Baltimore. He'd always believed there was another person behind those big glasses and big clothes she wore. When he saw her that night, wearing a tight red dress and contacts, with her yellow hair cascading around her shoulders, and behaving like a totally different person, he knew he had been correct. Calhoun Corners seemed to bring out the worst in Rayne Fegan and that night he had suspected he would meet the real Rayne.

But his friends had wanted to leave and he traveled

as part of a pack back then, so he hadn't even said hello to her. But the image of her in that little red dress, sipping wine, flirting with a circle of very interested men had stayed with him. For years. Actually, that image had given him something to think about when he wanted to steer his mind away from choking Brad Baker right after he'd run off with Jericho's live-in girlfriend.

He had to be honest with himself and admit the memory had morphed into a fantasy. But now that he knew the persona Rayne hid was that of a polecat, not a tigress, he would easily be able to shove down the stupid notion that he wanted to take off those glasses and loosen her hair.

"What did she want?"

Feeling like a man caught with his hand in a cookie jar, Jericho glanced at Greg. "Nothing."

"Oh, come on, Jericho!" Martha groaned. "There's no way Rayne Fegan would step foot in this office unless there was something so damned serious going on her in life that she couldn't get help elsewhere. Spill it!"

Jericho shook his head. He had absolutely no allegiance to Rayne Fegan. If anything, he and his family should be jumping for joy that her father was gone. Particularly since he'd left of his own volition. He wasn't hurt or kidnapped or even in any danger now that the loan shark had been paid by Rayne.

Just thinking her name made Jericho feel strange, but relegating his fantasy to the farthest corner of his brain, he remembered the forlorn look on her face when she realized it was possible her father would never come home. Mark Fegan might not be the only family Rayne had, but he was the parent who'd chosen to raise her. Her mother had made no secret of the fact that she didn't want a child tagging along with her to New York City. Six-year-old Rayne had seemed to take the situation in her stride. After all, staying in Calhoun Corners had meant keeping her friends, her home, her father.

But now that she'd alienated nearly everybody in town with her part in trying to unseat Jericho's dad, and her father was gone, so was all of Rayne's bluster. He couldn't exactly feel sorry for the girl who'd dedicated most of the past year to making his family miserable, but having been on the outs with his own family and having lost his best friend when Brad ran off with Laura Beth, Jericho understood what it was like to be alone. He wouldn't wish it on anybody.

Not even Rayne.

"It turns out that what she came in for isn't a police matter after all. There's no reason for me to brief you."

Martha groaned. Greg shook his head and went back to work on his report. Jericho returned to his office and forgot all about Rayne Fegan until he was striding along Main Street, on his way to the diner for lunch. He glanced down an alley and saw her walking up Second Street.

He stopped, watched her turn up Prospect Avenue, and frowned. She was walking to her house. *Walking?* It was freezing! His frown deepened. Her house was at the *top* of Prospect Avenue, which really should have been named Prospect Hill, because the entire avenue was a steep incline. It would take her at least most of her lunch hour just to walk to her house and back.

He shook his head. What did he care? Her dad owned the paper for which she worked and with him gone she was the boss. She could be a few minutes late returning from lunch.

Calling himself crazy, he finished the trip to the diner and chose a seat at a wooden table like the twenty or so others scattered about. A long shiny red counter matched the booths that circled the outside rim of the room. Red-and-white checkered curtains hung in evenly spaced intervals on the wall of windows beside the booths.

He ordered a chef salad and pulled out a copy of the *Calhoun Corners Chronicle.* If he weren't the chief of police, he wouldn't open Rayne's father's rag for all the tea in China. But he was the chief of police and it was prudent for him to keep up with births, deaths, weddings and engagements. Not to send cards and be in good "social" standing, but because a police department never knew when the change of a family's status would result in a strain that could culminate in a domestic disturbance. On the other hand, finding the right girl or becoming a father could also tame a usually drunk and disorderly twenty-year-old.

Elaine Johnson, the tall, amply built wife of the diner owner, Bill Johnson, walked over with his salad. She set the dish on his place mat.

"Thanks, Elaine."

"You're welcome, *Chief,*" she said, a giggle in her voice.

He glanced up and smiled. "Jericho's fine. I'm not much for titles."

"You should be," Elaine said, her brown eyes gleaming with pleasure. "Your mother is so proud of you. Nobody in your family even knew you'd gone into law enforcement. It was such a surprise."

"And exactly the opposite of what everybody expected."

She batted her hands in dismissal. "My guess is that you saw the inside of a jail one too many times and realized that if you didn't change you might find yourself locked up permanently."

Jericho grimaced. She was close but not exactly right. He'd actually made his first attempt at reforming at around twenty-three, when Laura Beth Salvatori came into his life. A tall, beautiful redhead, with a quick wit and a sharp mind, she was a challenge for his intellect as well as his sexual prowess. In the end, he'd won her over. Or so he'd thought.

After they lived together for two years, his best friend, Brad Baker, had come to Colorado for a visit. A rich kid Jericho had bummed around with on local ski slopes when Brad was in the Western United States and not in Europe, Brad was every bit as good-looking as Jericho, twice as charming and a thousand times richer. Laura Beth had taken one look at Brad and that was the end of anything she'd felt for Jericho. She'd packed her bags and left with Brad that weekend. That was the last Jericho had seen of Laura Beth or Brad and the beginning of what Jericho referred to as his lost years.

Hurt and angry, he drank, got fired from his manufacturing job and went back to bumming around the ski slopes, picking up enough money for booze and bail by giving skiing lessons. Then one night he woke up in jail with a teenage boy who had stabbed a rival gang member. They'd talked and Jericho realized that the kid hadn't had half the guidance and love Jericho had had in his formative years. He'd found himself telling the boy some of the very things his father had told him and by morning the kid had seen the error of his ways.

Unfortunately, the boy he had stabbed died during the night. The kid Jericho had saved wouldn't get a second chance. He would go to prison. Maybe for life.

That sunny morning when Jericho stepped out of jail, he realized he was drinking, getting into fights, gambling away his money, all because a woman he'd loved left with a guy he'd thought was his friend. At first, his behavior might have seemed justified, but two years later, he knew that if he continued down that path, Laura Beth really would have taken everything.

So he quit drinking—except for the occasional beer or glass of wine with dinner—and he'd had a long talk with his attorney who had convinced him to go into law enforcement. After graduating from the police academy, he'd spent almost five years working vice in Las Vegas. Then his dad offered him the job as chief of police in Calhoun Corners, and he knew it was time to come home.

"Whatever your reasons for going straight," Elaine was saying when Jericho came out of his thoughts. "Most of us are glad you're home."

Jericho smiled. He hadn't missed the "most" in her last statement. He knew he had detractors, people who thought his dad had been wrong to make him chief of police. People who assumed he hadn't changed or, worse, as the mayor's son he couldn't be objective. People who assumed that after Mark Fegan's attacks and the swell of people who believed the opinions in his ed- itorials, Ben Capriotti was getting his friends and family into position to make sure no one got so bold again. And now that Jericho thought about it, Mark leaving so mysteriously didn't look good for the Capriottis.

Elaine pointed at the paper. "Damn shame what happened at the *Chronicle.*"

Not sure what she meant, and not about to talk about anything Rayne had told him, Jericho didn't reply.

"I know. I know. You and your family aren't big fans of the paper but, really, once you get past Mark Fegan's rhetoric, it's the only source of news we have."

Jericho hid a smile. "You mean gossip."

She shook her head. "No. There's real news in there." She took the paper from his hand. "And Rayne doesn't shirk from the truth." She opened it to the page she wanted, folded it twice, and set in it front of Jericho so he could read the headline of the article at which she pointed.

"Newspaper to cut staff."

"Paper's not making money so she's going to run it single-handedly."

Jericho peered up at Elaine.

"Her dad's gone. There's no money. She can't afford to give out what little she makes to other people as salaries. So she's outsourcing the actual printing and distribution. And she'll do every other job herself."

Jericho stared at the article in disbelief. It was no wonder Rayne had been upset when she came into his office. Her life was a mess.

Before he could come up with an objective reply to Elaine about Rayne's circumstances, Drew Wallace, Jericho's sister Tia's new husband, entered the diner. Wearing his trademark black Stetson, jeans and a denim jacket, he didn't look nearly as prosperous as Jericho knew he was.

Elaine waved him back. "You should eat with your brother-in-law," she said when Drew walked over.

Jericho motioned to the seat across from him. "Sure, Drew, have a seat," he said, then Elaine scampered away to get a place mat and silverware.

As Drew pulled out the chair across from Jericho, he said, "So how's it going?"

"Good. How's Tia?"

Drew rolled his eyes. "Between doing her advertising job from our den, planning Rick and Ashley's wedding in our living room, getting ready for our baby in our bedroom and taking Ruthie every chance she can get, our house is a madhouse."

Jericho laughed.

"Yeah, you can laugh."

"Oh come on. You love it."

Drew scowled. "It's better than being alone."

"Right," Jericho said, knowing male bluster when he heard it. He'd said a few things like that a time or two himself when he was living with Laura Beth. He'd griped about stockings in the sink, telephone bills, and the home shopping network, but he'd loved having a woman around. He'd liked having an apartment that was a home, the scent of her cologne surprising him when he walked around corners, her warm body beside him on cold nights. But there was a downside to that, too.

Tia loved Drew exactly as he was. But to Laura Beth, Jericho had been something like a work in progress. She'd changed how he dressed, how he combed his hair and how he behaved. To keep her happy, he'd damned near let her turn him into a sap. But going into law enforcement had corrected that mistake. If a policeman looked weak at the wrong time, with the wrong person, he could find himself dead. So, Jericho was a strong, not-to-be-messed-with lawman, set in his ways, grouchy, cantankerous and glad to be.

"So what the hell is the deal with Rayne Fegan hiking up Prospect Avenue?"

Jarred out of his thoughts, Jericho looked up at Drew. "You saw her, too?"

"She's a wacky, wacky woman." Drew shook his head. "It's raining, but she has no umbrella and she's trudging up that hill as if she's got the weight of the world on her shoulders."

Jericho knew that to Rayne the weight of the world *was* on her shoulders, but he said nothing. He certainly wouldn't reveal what he'd been told in a police interview.

Drew opened the menu Elaine handed him before she set down place mats and utensils and walked away. "Of course, with a dad like hers, how could she be anything but wacky?"

Jericho took a breath. "I guess."

"The way he dogged your dad through this year's mayoral campaign was ridiculous." Drew caught Jericho's gaze. "You know he even brought up your past and Rick's."

"No. I didn't know that."

"He tried to get people to think that if your dad couldn't raise his own kids, he couldn't be trusted to run a whole town. But that backfired. Even if it wouldn't have been ridiculous to bring up things that happened fifteen years ago, Rick came home with a degree and took over Seven Hills as if he were born to it." Laughing, Drew shook his head. "And that angle fizzled pretty darned quickly."

"Yeah, Rick certainly came home a changed man," Jericho said, knowing that bringing up his past and Rick's past had been a last-ditch effort by Mark Fegan to save his hide from the loan shark. Jericho didn't wonder why somebody wanted his dad out of office. The horse farmers who made up about sixty percent of the local population were thrilled that Ben Capriotti had maintained ordinances that precluded big business from moving in and farmland from becoming housing developments. Twenty or thirty percent of the people who liked living in a safe, quiet small town also supported him. But some landowners, particularly heirs who wished to sell the farms they didn't want to run, weren't as supportive. Some were downright devious. And Mark Fegan had been a pawn.

"Your family is becoming something like a force in this town."

"Yeah," Jericho agreed, but not happily. Jericho's father had become mayor in the late seventies when the farmland was in danger of being swallowed up by developers. Now Drew Wallace, Jericho's brother-in-law, was one of the super-successful horse farmers who liked things the way they were. Even Rick fell into that category. Not only was he marrying Ashley Meljac, but Ashley's dad had deeded Seven Hills horse farm to Rick and Ashley as an engagement present. He stood to lose if anything in Calhoun Corners changed.

All that caused an unexpected problem for Jericho. He didn't have a vote on council, couldn't change ordinances or vote to keep them as they were, but he was the one who kept the peace. And that gave him a power of sorts. He had to answer to his dad, because his dad was the mayor. But he couldn't become a yes-man. He and his dad might laugh about the people who worried about Ben Capriotti hiring his own son to be chief of police, but Jericho knew he had to prove he was objective, not just to protect himself and his own reputation, but also to protect his dad's.

He might have inadvertently shot himself in the foot by so easily dismissing Rayne Fegan.

Chapter Two

At eight o'clock that night, after working a twelve-hour shift—still organizing the department and getting to know his officers—Jericho walked down the alley behind Main Street until he was at the back door of the newspaper office. He'd given Rayne the name of the best skip tracer he knew, so the search for her father was probably already under way. But that was as it should be. Hunting for a person who wasn't actually missing was out of his purview. Still, he couldn't let it appear that he had too casually dismissed Rayne. He knew how perception could be reality to some people, especially in a small town, so he had to nip speculation in the bud. One quick check to make sure everything was progressing would go a long way to prove he wasn't giving Rayne the brush-off because of their fathers' feud.

Jericho tried the door and was relieved to find it was locked. For as out-of-sorts as Rayne had seemed to be when she was at his office that morning, Jericho had worried that she might be too upset to think clearly. The locked door showed she was doing the important day-to-day things in her life, which meant she was fine. Nine chances out of ten when she saw him, she'd snipe at him. That would be complete proof that things were back to normal and once he followed through on the situation with her dad his duty would be done.

He knocked but no one answered. Having seen lights in the front part of the first-floor offices, he knew she or somebody was inside, so he knocked again. A few seconds later the door opened. Rayne frowned at him.

"Yes?"

"I wanted to see how things turned out when you called my friend."

"The skip tracer?"

He nodded.

She took a breath, then opened the door a little wider. "Come in."

Jericho almost groaned. If she'd called his friend and had good results, all she had to do was say yes. Her inviting him in was not a good sign. Damn.

"I called your friend," she said as she closed the door. She motioned for him to follow her through a path created between piles of boxes that were jammed in the room. Jericho had no clue what was inside the stacks of cardboard containers, and didn't ask as he navigated around them.

"But he's too expensive for me."

"Oh." In the hall just outside the box-filled room and before he would have stepped into the front room of the newspaper offices, Jericho stopped walking. "I forgot he charges a hefty fee."

"His fee's not that far out of line with the other private investigators I called, but I couldn't afford them, either." She took a breath and continued into the front room. "I paid all the money I had saved to the loan shark." She fell into the chair behind the desk next to the open door of an office Jericho assumed was her father's. "I didn't think any further ahead than getting that debt paid."

"Don't you have escrow or reserves here at the paper?"

She shook her head. "No. When I realized I would have to find my dad to tell him the debt had been paid, I looked at the books for the business."

"And?"

"And we are broke."

Jericho wasn't surprised that she so easily poured out all her troubles. The uniform he wore usually inspired trust. Especially in people who had no one else to talk to. But he'd fulfilled his responsibilities by giving her the skip tracer's name and since she couldn't afford the skip tracer, and he really didn't have the authority to help her, they were at a dead end. He stayed silent, not volunteering any more assistance.

"So anyway," she said with a note of finality in her voice, which was there, Jericho hoped, because she understood there was nothing more for them to discuss. "I don't have the money to hire your friend." She pushed her big glasses up her nose. "In case rumor hasn't reached you, I didn't even have the money to keep my own staff."

"Do you think your dad assumed you'd close the

paper once you saw the financial condition?" The question was out before Jericho could stop it. But it made sense. A person didn't abandon things they wanted saved.

Still, his question surprised them both so much that Rayne's gaze jumped to his. When her pretty blue eyes met Jericho's, a flash of memory of her in the contacts and the tight red dress leaped into his brain. He wasn't seeing the girl in the too big jeans and the ponytail, but the siren at the party.

"I can't close the paper." Her words came out little more than a whisper. "It's the only thing we have." She shook her head. "It's the only thing *he* has. If I close it, he'll never come back."

The sadness in her voice caused compassion to tighten Jericho's chest and he damned near cursed. He didn't like her. She didn't like him. Hell, she didn't like his whole damned family. He shouldn't feel sorry for her. But he couldn't stop thinking that he'd help the girl in the red dress—on his own time. His fertile imagination instantly came up with a thousand different ways she could repay him if he found her dad. But that was just plain wrong. Stupid. Macho. The kind of situation a smart law enforcement officer stayed away from.

She snorted derisively. "Look who I'm talking to. Your family hates mine. I'm the one who was digging up the dirt that my dad used in editorials before the election. My dad was the one writing the editorials. I understand why you don't want to help us."

"My decision not to help has nothing to do with disliking you or your dad. The department can't investigate a case where someone isn't really missing. This is

America. Your dad left a note saying he was going and he has a right to travel wherever he wishes."

"Whatever." She took a quick breath, then said, "Just go. Okay? I'm fine."

Jericho almost turned to leave, but couldn't quite do it. Having dismissed him, Rayne bent her head to return to her work and couldn't see him as he glanced at the empty chairs behind the desks and the pitch-black world beyond the big front windows. If the stack of papers piled to her right was any indication, Rayne would be burning the midnight oil tonight and every night. Alone in an empty office, in a downtown area that was deserted when the shops closed, knowing her dad had no clue that he could come home because she'd drained her own accounts to save him.

He took a breath. He refused to feel sorry for her. She'd just as soon spit at him as look at him. And anything he felt for her was nothing more than imagination. A fantasy.

Yet, somehow he couldn't leave.

"Oh, for heaven's sake," Rayne said, sighing with disgust. "What is it with men that when they see a woman with a bit of a problem they're absolutely positive she can't handle it alone? I'm fine. I'm betting I can even find my dad. I'm an investigative reporter, remember? Tracking down people and information is what I do."

"So you have contacts you can call at the Social Security Administration?"

"Yes."

"And did you call them?"

Rayne sighed heavily, as if put off by his question, but Jericho wasn't fooled.

"You called, but if your dad got a job, he's not using his social security number. I'm guessing you checked all your usual places and found nothing. That's why you came to me this morning. You had already used all your resources. I was your last resort."

"Do you think I would have come to you first?"

"No," he said, rubbing his hand along the back of his neck. She'd pursued all the normal avenues for leads and maybe even a few odd ones, trying to find her dad and she'd come up empty. That's why his instincts were telling him not to believe her bravado. He really was her last resort. And he couldn't help her.

"Rayne, I…"

"Just leave, okay?"

"I can't." He didn't know why but his feet didn't seem to want to move.

"You know what? I had a boyfriend like you, who thought I couldn't handle my own life. He didn't like my weight so he put me on a diet. He didn't like my glasses so I got contacts. He didn't like the way I dressed so he went shopping with me. He turned me into a completely different person."

Jericho said nothing, vividly remembering that person. The beautiful effervescent blonde he'd seen from across the room at a party.

"Before I knew it I was so dependent upon him that I was running to him for even simple decisions and when he left me I crumbled into an idiotic mass of hysteria. I will never be that woman again," she said, pointing at her chest. "I dress how I want. I don't diet. And I don't need anybody's help."

"Okay," Jericho said, suddenly understanding. Laura

Beth had tried to change him, too. He believed living with a manipulator had made him cantankerous, but Rayne took a more optimistic approach. She thought her run-in with a manipulator had made her independent. He could accept that, but because he understood her need to be her own person, it was doubly important that he back off. If he couldn't help her in his official capacity as chief of police, any assistance he gave would be something like charity, and independent people didn't accept charity.

"I'll go then."

"Great."

With that he turned and walked out of her office, through the back room cluttered with boxes and into the alley. He made his way down the dark corridor until he came to the side alley that led to Main Street. He turned right and jolted to a stop when he almost ran into Elaine as she bounded out the side door of the diner.

"Hey, Jericho," she said, coming to a quick halt so she didn't bump into his chest. "Are you on alley patrol tonight?"

He quickly said, "Something like that," then realized that he sounded exactly as he had when he was a teenager caught out after curfew. But tonight he had nothing to hide. No reason to cover the fact that he'd just been to Rayne Fegan's office. Actually, it was good that he'd checked up on Rayne. Even better that Elaine had caught him. If he explained himself, this time tomorrow everybody in town would know he had treated Rayne no differently than he would anybody else in town. His objectivity for his job would stand out like a neon sign.

"I saw the lights in the *Chronicle* offices and did a check. I figured Rayne Fegan was working late, but I stopped by anyway just in case something was wrong."

Elaine's smile grew. "You checked on her?"

"That's my job."

Elaine laid her hand on his forearm and caught his gaze. "Well, good for you."

Mission accomplished. Now he had no reason to check on Rayne tomorrow. No reason to get sniped at. No reason to be accused of hating her family. No reason to be in the same room with a woman who drove him crazy with an attraction that was all wrong. Dead wrong. She wasn't the woman he created in his fantasy. She wasn't even the woman he remembered. That woman was a passing fad for her. Or the product of a boyfriend's manipulation. From here on out he was staying away from Rayne Fegan and if at all possible he was forgetting what she looked like in that red dress.

As Rayne walked down Prospect Avenue the next morning, she saw Bert Minor, owner of the hardware store, parking his truck in front of the post office. Bert was one of the people who not only hadn't called to authorize her to put his longstanding ad in this week's edition of the paper, but also hadn't paid his bill for past ads.

She needed that money. Her dad had been paying his employees and their payroll taxes by taking cash withdrawals on one of his personal credit cards. She wasn't responsible for any of that debt, but she still had plenty of expenses. Utilities had to be paid, so did the printer. She hadn't bought gas for her car in a week. Unless advertisers began paying their bills, this time next week she might not be able to afford the cup of coffee that sustained her every morning until she could walk home and heat a can of soup—which she would eat for both lunch and supper.

She could buy a lot of soup with the four hundred dollars Bert owed her, but more than that she needed him to begin running his ad again so the money would continue.

Knowing she had just enough time to get down the hill before he retrieved his mail and returned to his truck, she quickened her steps. As she rounded the corner onto Main Street, he burst from the post office, hurrying to his vehicle to escape the chill.

Catching a sliver of his jacket sleeve, she stopped him. "Hey, Bert!"

"Hey, Rayne." The tall, round, hardware store proprietor ducked his head, refusing to meet her eyes. "I heard about the paper. Sorry."

"Yeah, well, just because I let my employees go that doesn't mean the paper's out of commission. So if you didn't call to authorize this week's ad because you think we're shutting down, you're in luck. *I'm* running the paper."

He peeked over at her. "You're running it?" he asked, sounding surprised.

She would have been insulted that he apparently didn't consider her able to take over, but Bert wasn't known for his tact. "Yes, Bert."

"But you don't have any management experience."

Deciding it wasn't out of line for the locals to want her to prove herself, she smiled at him. "What I don't have in experience, I make up for in brains."

He laughed. "Not a person in town can argue that you aren't smart."

"So? Can I run your ad?"

He glanced down. "Uh, I don't know, Rayne." He looked up and caught her gaze. "It's a small town. Everybody knows I own the hardware. Everybody knows where I'm located. I'm not having a sale." He shrugged. "No reason to run an ad."

"Everybody's always known who you are and where you are and what you sell, but you still took ads in the paper." She nearly reminded him that all the local businesses advertised more to support the paper than to draw in customers, doing their part to make sure the *Chronicle* didn't close. It was the same reason farmers in the area bought all their tractor parts and tools from him, to support him so that he would be there when they needed something in a pinch.

But she stopped herself because she suddenly got the picture. He wasn't running his ad because he didn't care about keeping the paper. He didn't care if she had to close down.

"I know I always had those ads, Rayne, but your dad was pretty hard on Ben Capriotti and Ben got elected and now his son is chief of police."

"And you're afraid of reprisal?"

Bert batted a hand. "Not even a little bit. Ben's a good man. He wouldn't cheat. And I'm not afraid of Jericho. If anything I think we're really lucky to have somebody with his background protecting our town."

She couldn't argue with Jericho's experience. When she was helping her dad try to oust Ben Capriotti, she'd checked into Jericho's life and discovered he was a well-respected member of the Las Vegas police department. Pressed for an opinion about Jericho's competence, she'd have to agree with Bert that Calhoun Corners was lucky to get him.

But she'd never considered the reprisal aspect. Because Ben had announced that he'd hired Jericho to replace Chief Nelson the same day that Rayne's dad had disappeared, she'd hardly paid any attention to the fact that Ben had hired his own son for a position that held a lot of power. For the past two weeks her focus had been on finding the loan shark and getting her dad's debt paid. Taking the time now to consider Ben giving his own son such an important job, Rayne didn't believe Bert had to worry about reprisal, but she did have to wonder about herself, the paper and even her dad if he ever came home.

But that was a worry for another day. Right now she had to focus on saving the paper.

"So if you're not concerned about Jericho or Ben, what's the deal? Why don't you want your ad?"

Bert shrugged. "I don't know. It just seems wrong to support you when you worked so hard to get a good guy out of office."

"Okay," Rayne said, agreeing because she didn't know what else to say. She couldn't tell him that her dad had brokered a deal to get Auggie Malloy elected as a way to pay a debt he'd made with a loan shark. She couldn't even tell Bert that she hadn't necessarily agreed with her dad that Ben Capriotti needed to be replaced. The truth was, she hadn't looked into the situation hard enough when she'd returned from Baltimore. Still upset by her breakup and happy to be with the one person she knew loved her as herself, she'd simply signed on for whatever her dad wanted.

The best she could do now was keep the paper going, return it to being the nonpartisan publication it was supposed to be and prove to Bert that it would be okay to run an ad again.

Squirming uncomfortably, Bert said, "I've gotta run."

Rayne nodded but Bert was already on his way to his truck. "Hey, Bert," she called, and he paused by a parking meter. "Just keep an open mind, okay?"

"Sure, Rayne," he said, but Rayne got the distinct impression his kind response was only lip service.

She turned to walk down the street. It was unfair that Bert wouldn't renew his ad, but she understood his reasoning. All the same, she began to shiver with the seeds of an emotion that felt very much like anger. Not toward the Capriottis who were beginning to look like innocent victims of her dad's bad investment. Not toward Bert who was being a thorn in her side, but who thought he had good reason. No. She was starting to feel angry with her dad.

She took a breath to calm herself. Being angry with her dad was wrong. Yes, he'd been difficult during the election. But newspaper editors had the right to question politicians in editorials. That had been going on since colonial days. And Ben Capriotti *had* had a heart attack. Her father had a responsibility to ask the voters to consider if Ben was still physically able to do the job as mayor. Her dad hadn't really done anything wrong.

Stepping inside the diner for a cup of coffee to take to the office so she didn't have to waste the grounds for an entire pot, she saw Jericho sitting at the counter.

She could easily envision him fitting in the police force of a big city. She could understand how the excitement of a fast-paced place like Vegas had attracted him. He had always been the kind of guy who wanted something bigger and better than what Calhoun Corners had to offer, yet he had come home. And Rayne had to wonder why. Had he taken a job as chief of police of his little hometown because he suddenly wanted a quieter, more settled life? Or had he come home to get revenge for his dad?

Her conscience tweaked. Jericho had been kind to her when she'd come to his office. He'd listened to her story like a professional, and he'd even given her dad the benefit of the doubt. Then he'd checked up on her to see if she'd hired the skip tracer.

She drew a quiet breath. All right. From the way Jericho had handled this situation so far, she had to admit it didn't seem as if he had come home to carry out a grudge against her dad. But that didn't mean there was any reason to go overboard about him and the way he'd treated her. Sure, he'd checked up on her. Going above and beyond the call of duty since it wasn't his job. And, yes, he'd spoken kindly about her dad, giving him the benefit of the doubt when people like Bert didn't. But that didn't make him good or even nice.

She frowned. If none of those made him nice, then why had he done them? Why had he milled around her office, upset that there was nothing he could do to help her?

Unless he'd felt sorry for her?

She nearly groaned out loud. For Pete's sake! That was worse than his teasing when she was in grade school! Her dad was gone. The family business was in trouble. She didn't have a dime to spare. And the local chief of police, the man she used to have a killer crush on, felt sorry for her. She was, quite literally, at the lowest point in her life.

When she got to the end of the counter, where the cash register sat, she pretended she didn't see Jericho as Elaine came scrambling over. "Hey, good morning!"

"Good morning, Elaine. Just a cup of coffee."

"No Danish?"

She shook her head and smiled. "Nope. Dieting."

As she said the words her cheeks flamed with color. Not because it was a lie. Though it was. She'd love to have a Danish, but couldn't afford to spend a dollar on a pastry. Her face flushed with embarrassment because Jericho Capriotti was within hearing distance and the night before she'd told him that she'd vowed never to diet again.

"Dieting!" Elaine gasped. "You're thin as a rail!"

Positive Jericho would make some kind of smart remark about her having said she'd never diet again, Rayne was relieved when he didn't comment. He didn't even look in her direction.

She relaxed a bit and laughed. "Elaine, you worry like an old woman."

"I am an old woman. Any word about your father?"

Tears flooded her eyes and Rayne nearly cursed. Of all the times to pick to get weepy about her father, this was the worst. She didn't want to cry in front of Jericho—who already felt sorry for her. Hell, she didn't want to cry in front of anybody. She was a twenty-four-year-old woman who should be completely capable of handling a crisis. And she was. If this were a simple matter of taking over a failing paper she'd just do what needed done. But this wasn't a simple matter of taking over a nearly bankrupt business. Her dad might not be lost or kidnapped or even in danger now that she'd paid off his debt, but he was gone. And she missed him.

She sucked in a breath. "No word."

Elaine caught Rayne's forearm, drawing her gaze to hers. "He'll be okay."

Rayne forced a smile. "Yeah," she said, then batted her hand in dismissal. "I'm sure he's fine."

She paid for her coffee and stepped out into the crisp morning air. Walking to the offices for the *Calhoun Corners Chronicle,* she straightened her shoulders. She'd fought worse battles, harder fights, and she'd lived. What made this one different was that she wasn't only alone, she was broke. So broke she had to worry that the utilities would be shut off at her house and she'd end up sleeping on the leather sofa in her dad's office. So broke she was surviving on soup.

Reminding herself of her dire straits actually made her stronger and she hastened her steps to get out of the cold. She wasn't going to wait for the accounts that owed money to "decide" to pay. She would call them. She needed to cover the paper's expenses and to pay the utilities at her dad's house. If everybody brought their accounts current, she might even have a couple dollars left over for food. She didn't have to do anything except write the copy for the newspaper, create the ads and pay the bills. She'd take this one step at a time. One ad at a time. One article at a time. One bill at a time. And who knew? Maybe one day her dad would see the paper was still in operation, and he'd contact her and she could tell him he could come home.

* * *

At eleven o'clock, Rayne's coffee was long gone and her stomach was officially growling. But she told herself to go back to work to get her mind off her hunger and picked up the receiver of the phone to make another call to one of the advertisers who owed her money.

Before she dialed the final digit of the phone number, she heard a sound. Dull and muffled, it wasn't easily identified. She stopped dialing and listened again. This time the sound came through a little clearer. Someone was knocking at her back door.

Confused, she rose from her office chair and made her way through the maze of boxes in the back room. She opened the door and saw Jericho Capriotti standing in the alley.

Wearing his police uniform with heavy jacket to keep out the cold, he looked strong and capable, and the first thought that jumped into her mind was that she would have killed for this kind of attention from him in her teen years. Unfortunately the second thought was that he felt sorry for her.

"What do you want?"

He drew a breath. "I got to thinking about your dad—"

"I thought you said this wasn't a police matter?"

"It isn't. But we're not exactly swamped over at the borough building and I got to thinking about your dad—"

She had no idea why he had been thinking about her dad, but she did know it wasn't because he had just popped into Jericho's head. "I don't need your pity."

He sighed heavily, then glanced to the right. As he

did that Rayne noticed that he carried a brown paper bag. At the same time her nose caught the scent of something wonderful. Warm bread. Her stomach growled, just as the wind gusted, and Rayne prayed Jericho hadn't heard.

"Look, I don't feel sorry for you. I do need something to do. We can't make this official but unofficially there are things I can try." He smiled slowly and held up the brown paper bag. "And I sort of figured you might be suspicious or unfriendly, so I brought a peace offering. I got Elaine to make roast beef sandwiches on freshly baked bread."

Rayne's stomach growled again.

"Aha. You can't say you aren't hungry."

She was starved. Absolutely starved. And if the sandwich smelled any better she'd eat it without taking it out of the paper bag. Still, if she believed he was being honest and fair with her about his inability to help her look for her dad, then he was here because he felt sorry for her. She couldn't accept charity.

"I was just about to break for lunch—"

"Good," Jericho said, making a move to step into the back room, but she put her hand on his chest to stop him. Pinpricks of awareness danced up her arm. She was touching him. After decades of having a crush on him, she was finally touching him…and it was to block him from getting into her building. Her life just sucked.

"I was on my way to my house to open a can of soup."

"A sandwich is better."

She gaped at him. "Soup is better on a cold day."

"Whatever. Look, I'm going to do some cursory investigating for your dad whether you help me or not. If you let me in you can give me some direction. If you don't and I start cold, nine chances out of ten I won't find him." He caught her gaze. "Is that what you want?"

He knew how badly she wanted to find her dad, so he also knew he had her. She took a long breath and blew it out slowly. "I want him found so we can tell him I paid off his debt."

"That's what I thought."

He stepped into the back room and Rayne turned her back on him, leading him into the office area. She walked to her desk and sat on her chair as he took the seat behind the desk across the aisle in front of hers.

"I got this week's edition of the paper."

Rayne took a breath. "It's a little small."

"Paper's never been big," he said causally as he handed a roast beef sandwich across the aisle to her.

Her pride desperately wanted her to refuse it. Her common sense knew she couldn't. As casually as he handed it, she reached for it.

"I also brought coffee."

"I could have made a pot."

He brushed her off. "This is simpler. I only have a half hour for lunch." He caught her gaze. "Basically, I'm doing this on my own time. It can't be official."

Mesmerized by his beautiful green eyes, Rayne was struck again by how unfair her life was. Here was the man she had always wanted and instead of being able to put her best foot forward she was a needy fool with an irresponsible father.

Gripping the container of coffee he handed her, Rayne said, "I'm not sure what you want from me."

Jericho finished chewing the bite of sandwich he'd

taken before he said, "First, I'm assuming you did the usual checks of things like his credit cards to see if he'd used them."

Unwrapping her sandwich, Rayne nodded. "He hasn't used them."

"Do you think he had any secret, private credit cards you don't know about?"

With the scent of roast beef wafting to her nose, Rayne shook her head. "Not unless they're under an alias."

Jericho brightened. "Did he have aliases he used to get stories?"

She laughed. "No. At least none that I knew of. My dad didn't even cover regular stories anymore, let alone do undercover work."

"But he did at one time?"

"He was a very well-respected journalist in D.C."

"No undercover work then?"

Rayne frowned. "You know, he only ever talked about his beginnings at the *Wall Street Journal* and then his time at the White House before he took over the *Chronicle* for my mother's family. If there was something he did in between those two, he never mentioned it."

"That would be a good place for you to start looking. See if you can find out what he did in between those two jobs or who his contacts were at the last job he held." Jericho paused. "You're not eating. Don't you like roast beef?"

"I love it."

"Then eat. I've got to be back in a few minutes and we need to get as much done as we can."

Rayne glanced down at the sandwich then across the

aisle at him. Though it was hard, she quietly said, "Thanks."

"Hey, you're welcome. As I said, I was bored. Looking for your dad will be a good way to keep up my investigative skills."

He dismissed the sandwich so easily that Rayne almost believed it really was the afterthought he intended her to think it was. She took a bite of sandwich and struggled not to groan as the flavor exploded in her mouth.

"You said you had checked to see if he's using his social security number."

She nodded. "My dad's broke, but he's also a planner. So, I can't believe he just left without having a job to go to. Which means his social should have activity, but it doesn't."

"Which brings us back to the probability that he's using an alias."

Taking another bite of her sandwich, Rayne nodded. "Oh, this is good."

"It's the homemade bread," Jericho said, again casually.

But Rayne knew the sandwich tasted like heaven because it was manna from heaven. Having eaten nothing but canned soup for a week, she was starving.

And Jericho was the only one in town who had seen that.

"If you're really looking for my dad," she said, trusting him a little more, "you should also know that he put the payroll for the last two months on a credit card, along with the taxes. This month's bill for that card hasn't come in, but I'm guessing there will be another cash advance against it."

Jericho grimaced. "Ouch! That's going to be a hefty balance."

She nodded. "It also means he had a grub stake for leaving."

"And that he left you with another debt."

She shook her head. "Credit card's in his name, not the *Chronicle*'s. I'm not responsible for it."

"You may not be responsible, but if the creditors get nasty enough you might be forced to sell your dad's house to settle his scores."

She shook her head. "He put the house in my name a few months ago."

"He certainly made sure his ducks were in a row."

"I told you he was a planner."

She watched Jerico absorb all that. From the look on his face, his next comment didn't surprise her.

"Rayne, he walked away from a business, gave away his house." He caught her gaze. "It almost seems that he doesn't want to be found."

"Of course he doesn't! He thinks the loan shark is after him, but I paid that debt. He can come home."

"You might have paid the loan shark, but your dad still owes what's on that credit card. He no longer owns his house. He abandoned the paper." He caught Rayne's gaze and held it. "If he put his affairs in this much order, the rest of his plan could be equally detailed. You need to face the possibility that we aren't going to find him."

Chapter Three

That night Rayne was too sick at heart to eat the second half of the sandwich Jericho had brought her for lunch. She tried to eat it for breakfast the next morning, but it was no use. Her dad wasn't coming home and he'd planned it. He'd planned never to see her again.

She could understand his running from a debt and even abandoning a little newspaper that was failing, if only because he was tired of being a failure. But she could not understand his leaving her.

She listlessly dressed in her usual blue jeans and T-shirt, but knowing she'd have to turn down the thermostat in the newspaper offices, she also pulled on a heavy sweater. She walked to the *Calhoun Corners Chronicle* building even forgoing coffee at the diner. At her desk, she began organizing her notes for a day of writing articles about the lives of the residents of her small town and placing telephone calls to businesses hoping to get them to buy advertising or pay the bills for last month's ads.

She had just finished organizing her work when she heard the muffled knock at the paper's back door again. Confused, she glanced at the clock, thinking the guy who usually knocked should be at work himself. Then she realized Jericho might have good news about her dad.

She bounced from her chair and ran through the maze of boxes in the storage room and yanked open the door.

Jericho stood before her wearing jeans, a plaid work shirt and a leather jacket. His hair had been cut and was now too short to be tossed by the wind that raced down the corridor created by the backs of the buildings of Main and Second streets. His green eyes were wary, cautious, but he looked so sexily male that Rayne caught her breath.

Before she could stop herself, she said, "You don't have good news."

"I don't have any news." He waved a brown paper bag. "I brought coffee and doughnuts because I have to ask a favor."

It stung that she was so desperate, and her pride swelled defensively. "You don't have to bribe me with food."

"No. But it never hurts to be in a person's good graces when you ask for permission to look through her dad's office."

Her mouth fell open slightly.

"You and I realized yesterday that your dad had carefully planned his disappearance and that he's probably using an alias. So our only recourse now is to hope he left something behind in his office. Something that will give us a clue about where he went or what name he's using."

After the way they had left things the night before, Rayne had thought Jericho was done investigating. But he'd never actually said he was through, only that her dad might not be found. She didn't know whether to be relieved he had returned or depressed because looking through her dad's office was a fool's errand, but she wasn't going to tell him no.

"Come in."

She moved away from the door and Jericho stepped inside. "You don't sound very enthused."

Leading him to the main room, Rayne said, "You also mentioned yesterday that my dad probably doesn't want to be found. He might have his loan shark paid off, but he left behind the credit card debt and a failing business."

"He also left you behind."

Ignoring the pain in her heart, Rayne flippantly said, "Yeah, he sure did, and rather easily." ·

"You know," Jericho said, setting the brown paper bag on the desk across the aisle from hers. "We've been making a lot of assumptions about your dad because that's what investigators do. But one wrong conclusion can spiral until we're going so far in the wrong direction we're nowhere near the truth. So though it's okay for us to realize that your dad may not want to be found in order that we don't get our hopes up too high, we still have to work with what we have."

"A credit card debt and a failing business."

"No, we have fear of a loan shark and a daughter he was trying to protect."

"Protect?"

"Sure, he put his house in your name to assure that

he didn't leave you out in the cold. A man doesn't protect a daughter he wants to lose. We can't dismiss the possibility that he wants to come home, but he thinks he can't. That makes it more important than ever that we find him."

Feeling her spirits brighten, Rayne smiled. "I'd like to think that."

"Good. Eat this."

She glanced down at the chocolate doughnut he was handing her.

"Chocolate stimulates production of endorphins. I want you happy so that if I find something I need to ask you about you'll be thinking positively."

She laughed.

Jericho laughed, too.

But when they stopped laughing and she caught his gaze, the mood shifted. Staring into his eyes, she felt like the adult version of herself standing face-to-face with the adult version of the rebel she had so loved when he was just out of high school, bumming around, thumbing his nose at authority by refusing to go to college. The dynamic of their conversation had changed too quickly for him to control his reaction and she saw something in his eyes that she'd never thought she'd see back then. He found her attractive.

Attractive? In her blue jeans and bulky sweater? With her hair in a ponytail and her big glasses always falling off her nose?

She didn't think so.

Until she looked into his eyes again and there it was, as plain as day. Attraction. Her skin became hot and prickly. His breathing shifted. The color of his eyes sharpened. Difficult as it was for Rayne to fathom, they had chemistry.

He cleared his throat and turned away, reaching for the second cup of coffee he'd set on the desk. "This is yours, too."

She smiled. "Thanks."

"You're welcome." He waited a heartbeat then he said, "Do you want to come into your dad's office with me while I search or would you rather wait out here?"

She nearly told him she wanted to be with him as he rummaged around in her dad's desk and closets, but just as quickly she stopped herself. The idea of them having some sort of chemistry was too new to her, and with the way her emotions had been stretched to the limits lately, she couldn't risk that she'd say or do something totally foolish.

She caught his gaze again. "You go."

Jericho nodded and walked into Rayne's dad's office. As with everything else at the newspaper, the little room was crowded and cramped. Papers were stacked everywhere. Copies of magazine and newspaper articles had been clipped and sat in a bin by the big metal desk. Dust clung to the metal lamp bowed over the desk blotter. A knotted cord bulged from the phone.

Jericho sat on the wooden captain's chair behind the desk and it creaked. He shook his head. This did not feel right. Well, actually, that wasn't true, either. The office "felt" exactly the way he would presume the office of a man who had escaped would feel. There was an air of desperation in the room. Unfinished work sat everywhere. The phone was outdated, the desk old, the chair hard and unyielding. With surroundings as uncomfortable as these, Jericho could easily understand why Mark Fegan had no compunction about leaving.

Rather than flip on a desk lamp, Jericho rose and opened the blinds on the side-by-side windows behind the desk. Dust burst from the slats of the blind as they separated and danced in the incoming light. Stifling a cough, he batted it away, then took the seat again.

Opening the drawer on the lower right side of the desk, he heard Rayne talking on the phone. Polite and professional, she reminded the person she had called that he owed her money. Jericho stopped the movement of the squeaky drawer, listening to her plea. She didn't come across as desperate or even needy. She sounded like a business owner asking for payment of an overdue account, even as she tried to wheedle a new ad sale. By the way she said goodbye, Jericho knew she didn't believe she'd been successful on either score.

He took a quiet breath and returned his attention to the desk drawer. After the moment they'd had in Rayne's office, he knew it wasn't wise to be around her so much. But he couldn't help it. He couldn't turn away a person who was struggling. He knew what it was like to be alone and hungry.

Rifling through the contents of the drawer, he reminded himself that her finances weren't his concern and neither were her personal battles. Even if the town lost its little newspaper, that wasn't his worry, either. And if he didn't watch himself, he was going to get himself into trouble.

He picked up a tape recorder he found buried under two file folders, rewound the tape and listened to Mark Fegan dictating what sounded like a to-do list. He turned it off and set it on the desk so he could pull the pad and pen from his shirt pocket, then he turned it on again and wrote the list as Mark dictated it.

All of the items were instructions he would be giving to different members of his staff, such as creating ads and following up on stories. Though nothing seemed noteworthy or connected to Mark's disappearance, Jericho returned the tablet to his shirt pocket. He would more closely study the list later.

Trying to focus on the contents of the drawer, Jericho's attention was again caught by Rayne's voice.

"Hey, Mom, it's me."

He straightened in his seat.

"I know it's been a long time since I called," she continued, sounding as if she were leaving a message on an answering machine, "but I've been kind of busy. Especially since Dad left two weeks ago. He wrote a note, but didn't say where he was going and I was just wondering if he'd contacted you." She paused. "If he has, would you give me a call? My number is…" She recited her number and Jericho leaned back in his chair, once again feeling very odd.

Years ago, when Jericho had made his escape from Calhoun Corners, he'd left his family. They hadn't deserted him. At the very point in his life when he had all of his roaming out of his system, his dad had called him and asked him to come home. He had even given him a job.

Conversely, Rayne's mom hadn't wanted her. She made no bones about it. She made no excuses, save to say that some women weren't cut out to be mothers. She left her daughter with a dad who loved her, but her dad had never remarried, so Rayne had no siblings. At least none that Jericho knew of. She only had her dad. Was it any wonder that when her dad lead her down a path she followed?

Jericho shook his head, telling himself that her personal problems weren't his concern, but a little voice inside his head disagreed. His family might have very good reason to mistrust Rayne, but his secret crush on her after the party in Baltimore had sustained him through some ugly times. Now here she sat in the worst position of her life and he had the knowledge that could probably help her. If he were the kind to believe in fate, then he would almost have to assume she was the reason he had been brought home.

It might sound stupid. It might even sound egotistical, but no matter how many times or ways he tried to argue himself out of helping her, he felt called to help her and he refused to think it was because he wanted to sleep with her.

Although he did. He *really* did. Any man who had seen her with all that floating blond hair, wearing a red dress that fit like a glove, would want to sleep with her. But that made his fantasy irrelevant. The flesh-and-blood woman he felt called to help wasn't the woman he remembered from all those years ago. If finding Mark Fegan seemed like his destiny or a duty, it was for reasons other than his foolish crush.

He weeded through another eight or ten items in Mark Fegan's desk and found several old airline tickets. The stubs for Vegas, Miami and Des Moines caught his attention, if only because they demonstrated Mark's travel choices were eclectic. They also proved Mark had been to those places and would be familiar with them. Even a brief visit would give him a sense of security about any one of them.

Jericho strode into the front office. "Do you mind if I make copies of these?"

Without looking up, Rayne shook her head. "Nope. Go ahead."

And Jericho relaxed. He had nothing to worry about. He might be attracted to a memory, but he wasn't attracted to *her.* And she appeared to have zero interest in him. Sure, they had a little eye contact that morning, but that was a fleeting…something. Fleeting being the operative word. As long as he controlled himself, he would have no problem helping her.

"I'd also like to make a copy of the note if I can."

She glanced up. "Why?"

"I have a friend who owes me a favor. He has a friend who analyzes handwriting. That guy could tell us if your dad wrote the note under duress."

"Under duress?"

"It's a long shot, given the way your dad's personal life was put in order before he left. But I think it might be a good idea to rule out that your dad was taken against his will."

She opened the center drawer of her desk and handed the notepad containing her dad's goodbye explanation to Jericho. "Here."

Jericho took it. "I'll also need a copy of something with a sample of you dad's normal handwriting."

She rummaged through some files on her desk, then pulled out a handwritten instruction sheet and handed that across the desk, too.

"Okay," Jericho said, catching her gaze. The look of longing he saw in her eyes caused the electricity that had arced between them earlier to return. The feeling tightened his chest again, stealing his breath, and he nearly cursed. He couldn't—absolutely couldn't—be falling for this woman. She was younger than he was. His family hated her family. Hell, her family had out and out persecuted his dad. For all practical intents and purposes he shouldn't even be helping her.

"Once I copy this I'm going to the diner for lunch with my dad." He knew exactly why he'd told her that. He wanted to remind her that they had differences and she shouldn't look at him with yearning in her eyes and he shouldn't be responding. "Can I bring something back for you?"

The expression in her eyes changed. Jericho saw it and he wanted to kick himself. She didn't have any money. He knew that. Yet he put her in the position where she had to lie or come up with a logical excuse.

She smiled and held his gaze with eyes that dared him to contradict her when she said, "No thanks. I like walking to my house at noon. It's good exercise."

"So, rumor has it that Mark Fegan ran away because he owed money to a loan shark."

Sitting at the diner, finished with his stew, Jericho glanced up at his dad. With salt-and-pepper hair and piercing brown eyes, Ben Capriotti was an impressive man.

"Are you kidding me?"

"So it's not true? He doesn't owe money. There was no note—"

"Dad, I don't want to talk about this with you."

"Ah, it's part of an investigation."

"I didn't say that."

"So you're not searching for him."

"I didn't say that, either."

"Well, what are you saying? I'm the mayor. The guy who was harassed for an entire election year by the guy who is missing. Do you know how this looks for me?"

"It shouldn't look like anything. The gossip doesn't involve you at all. Nobody's accusing you of running him out of town." He smiled at his dad. "So, it doesn't seem as if you have any reason to be concerned."

Ben sighed. "I would just like to know what the hell got into that guy that he went after me the way he did."

"He was always after you in one way or another."

"But not like this. And if it affects my town, I feel I need to know."

"Well, suffice it to say, it doesn't."

"So you do know?"

"Stop, Dad!"

"Rumor also has it that the paper is closing."

Jericho shook his head. His father wasn't somebody accustomed to taking orders. So there was no point in trying to get him to stop talking. "You know what everybody else knows. Rayne cut back out of necessity…"

One of Ben's eyebrows arched. "Rayne? You're talking an awful lot like a guy who's a little closer to the enemy than he was this time two days ago."

Jericho sighed, not really sure what to say. His dad was right. Two days ago he would have just as soon faced an angry mob than talk with Rayne Fegan. Yet today, when she'd looked at him with her defiant blue eyes, trying to make him believe she was fine, he didn't know whether to shake her silly or kiss her. And that scared him. His fantasy Rayne was morphing into the real Rayne and that was just plain wrong. The real Rayne was a polecat. She might be down right now, but she most certainly wasn't out. When she pulled herself up by her bootstraps—and he had no doubt that she would—there was no guarantee she'd even remember he'd helped her, let alone appreciate it.

"Are you working with her to help her find her dad?"

"Not officially."

"Why not?"

"Because he's really not 'missing.' He left a note saying he was going. Leaving town is not a crime. But just in case he was the victim of foul play, I copied the note this morning and faxed it to a crime lab in Vegas."

His dad gaped at him. "You called in a favor?"

Jericho drew a breath. He'd certainly hanged himself with that admission. He quickly tried to figure out a way to make it sound like a smaller deal than it was, but he couldn't think of anything.

Luckily, his dad didn't wait for an answer. "Jericho, I know you feel that you need to prove yourself. I can also guess that as a detective, finding the missing newspaper editor who just happened to be your dad's nemesis might appear to be the perfect way to show the whole town that you're not just smart, you're also objective. But watch these people. Mark Fegan's a snake. He was teaching his daughter to be a snake."

"She's also a resident with a dad who left under questionable circumstances. You're the one who taught me that real men don't run from hard jobs. I'm only doing what you taught me."

"Okay, fine. You might prove yourself to be smart and unbiased if you find him. But you'll also bring home a guy who will make your life miserable."

Jericho laughed. "Once I prove myself, he can't really make my life miserable."

"Oh really?" Ben asked, shifting on the booth seat. "I give him two weeks after you find him before he gets cocky."

"So what?"

"So he can't do anything to me. I'm elected. I'm in for four years. But you're an easy mark. He'll investigate what you did for the past ten years, find every damned mistake you made—including spending several nights in jail—and make you look foolish."

"Or prove that I've changed."

"You're such an optimist. These people aren't to be trifled with, Jericho."

The whole hell of it was Jericho knew his dad was right. The Fegans had been nothing but trouble. But something kept telling him that he couldn't desert Rayne. She needed somebody and right now he was the only somebody with the skill and training and connections to help her. He wasn't doing this to prove himself. He wasn't doing this to show people he'd changed or that he was smart or even that he could be objective. He was helping Rayne because something in his gut told him he had to.

He rationalized that his instincts were telling him that because there was nobody else to help her, but when he kept remembering her pretty blue eyes, the way her hair floated around her when she let it down, the way she smiled, he knew that wasn't true. He wasn't looking for Mark Fegan to prove himself or to help a woman who had no one else, he was helping her because he was beginning to like her and that was wrong. Not because the Fegans weren't trustworthy, as his dad had suggested. But because Jericho was losing his objectivity. Mark Fegan hadn't broken any laws in the town in which Jericho had jurisdiction. He had a right to leave. Jericho had to keep his wits about him and not go overboard in this search.

He returned to the newspaper offices and didn't bother knocking on the old wooden door. "I'm back," he called, making his way through the maze of boxes in the rear room. Stepping into the office section, he found Rayne busily working at her desk. He didn't ask her if she'd gone home to have lunch. He wasn't sure she would tell him the truth anyway.

Without looking up from her work, she said, "Hey."

"Anything interesting happen while I was gone?"

For that she did glance up, a puzzled smile on her face. "No."

He shrugged. "You never know. Your dad could have called."

She returned her attention to work and Jericho returned to Mark Fegan's office to continue to rifle through the man's possessions. Unfortunately, over the course of the afternoon he found so many old airline tickets, travel magazines and calendar entries of places Mark Fegan had visited that he knew Rayne's dad was a frequent traveler. He could go anywhere and fit in.

At three-thirty his cell phone rang. Glancing at the Caller ID, he saw it was Martha Wissinger from the police station.

He said, "Yeah, Martha."

"You got the oddest fax," she said without preamble. "It's from some guy in Vegas. It says, 'Reviewed note, nothing to lead me to believe it was written under duress. My guess is this guy just walked away.' And that's it."

Jericho rubbed his hand across his forehead. "That's what I thought."

"So it makes sense?"

"Yeah, thanks, Martha."

"Well, you're welcome, though I'm not sure what for."

Jericho hung up the phone with a resigned sigh, pushed himself out of the chair behind Mark Fegan's desk and walked out to the main room. "Rayne?"

Working very hard to school her expression, Rayne glanced up at Jericho. They'd had two "moments" that morning. Two times when their gazes caught and clung for just a second or two too long, and that wasn't right. She might have been half in love with this man for most of her life, but they weren't right for each other. Even if they were, their families were feuding. She would not, absolutely would not, let her feelings for him show again. Not just to protect herself. To protect him, too. He had been kind enough to help her. She wouldn't thank him by putting him in the awkward situation of knowing she had an enormous crush on him.

"I got the results from the handwriting analysis."

"And?"

"And my friend didn't think there was anything unusual. It's his opinion the note was not written under duress."

That did not surprise her, and she was also glad that her father apparently hadn't met with foul play, but her throat was suddenly tight and dry so she only nodded.

"There's more not-so-good news."

Hearing pity in his voice and hating it, Rayne cleared her throat and forced herself to speak. "You can say bad news. I can handle it."

"I found evidence that your dad has been to at least a hundred cities on three continents."

She shrugged. "He liked to travel."

"That means he's very comfortable traveling. Comfortable in new places. Not only could he have decided to settle in one of the cities he's visited, but he would know how to blend in."

"So, he's not going to be found?"

"Not without a lot of searching."

She took a breath. Jericho said nothing.

Finally she caught his gaze. "And the thing you're not saying is that you're done."

"I told you I had a little time to devote to helping you. That, if nothing else, we could eliminate the possibility that your dad had met with foul play."

"And you're convinced that possibility has been eliminated."

"Very convinced."

"And you're done?"

He nodded and she saw it again. The damned pity. Only two hours before this they'd shared a chemistry strong enough that she'd felt the need to come up with a plan for protecting him, but now it was gone and in its place was condescension.

Anger bubbled up inside her. She hadn't forgotten that he'd just gone to lunch with his dad, though she had for some unknown reason believed he wasn't going to be a puppet, doing his father the mayor's bidding.

"Well, how do you like that. You come in here this morning like a knight in shining armor, acting all big and bad like you're going to figure this thing out, but after one hour with your dad you're suddenly done."

"I didn't come in his morning thinking I would 'figure this thing out.' I wanted to make sure we weren't dismissing this too easily."

"But you wouldn't do it officially. Only unofficially."

He closed his eyes, as if completely frustrated. "I would think that my taking personal time to help you would mean something. I can't do anything about the fact that the evidence points to your dad leaving. He didn't just walk away from a debt to a loan shark. He also walked away from a business that was failing. A business he probably felt he couldn't save. Lots of men would have walked away for a lot less."

"He doesn't know that he can come home!"

"He would if he'd pick up the phone. Any time he wants to he can call."

The room became unbearably quiet as Jericho grabbed his hat and headed for the hall leading to the back room. When he reached the threshold, he stopped and faced her. "By the way, you're welcome."

Rayne swallowed as the slamming door shook her

office. Well, she wouldn't be wasting any more lunch hours wondering how she could protect him from their chemistry.

Chapter Four

The next morning Rayne walked into the diner with five cents over the exact amount of money for a cup of coffee. She strode to the counter. "Good morning, Elaine."

Elaine turned from the order window. "Hello, sugar. What'll it be?"

"Just coffee."

"I have some delicious sweet rolls."

Rayne smiled. "You know I'm dieting."

Elaine huffed out a breath. "Kids. In my day a little bit of meat on the bones was a good thing."

"It doesn't matter," Rayne said with a laugh. "I'm not hungry anyway."

"Suit yourself," Elaine said, handing the takeout cup of coffee to Rayne. "I'll see you tomorrow morning."

Rayne smiled and said, "See you tomorrow," though she knew there was no way in hell she could come back the next day. Even if she got a check or two in the mail, she wouldn't be able to draw on them until two days after they were deposited. That was the second thing she'd discovered after she'd taken over the newspaper. A check had arrived, looking like a blessing, but when she tried to get even fifty dollars cash, the teller had told her that there was a note on the account that all checks were to be held. So she had this coffee in her hand, five cans of soup, some macaroni, and the precious half can of coffee grains she kept in the office in case she got a visitor. Every day she didn't get a check was another day she'd be hungry.

Pushing open the door, she walked out into the cold morning just in time to see Jericho Capriotti opening the door of the borough building. She wanted to be angry with him for giving up on finding her dad, but she couldn't be. Jericho had sacrificed his day off to check into her dad leaving and he'd discovered what Rayne already knew to be true. Her dad was an avid traveler, so familiar with the country that he could go anywhere with an assumed name and blend in. She couldn't even be angry with Jericho for reminding her that her dad could call any time he wanted. The truth was the truth. Her dad could call, if he wanted to. Apparently, he didn't want to.

But that was exactly why she was upset with him and why she was going to do some serious thinking that morning. If he really didn't want to come back, then maybe she was making a mistake keeping the paper open. She had no money. No food. No grub stake to get her set up in another town. It was time to quit pretending that her dad would return if he knew the loan shark had been paid. She needed to update her résumé and begin looking for another job. If she didn't soon do something, she could find herself in Calhoun Corners starving forever.

Unless her dad's accounts began to pay. Then there would be money enough to run the paper and money enough to keep up the expenses on her house. She would be the publisher of a newspaper. Small, sure. But it was still a voice, a forum. She would be an entrepreneur.

And as for her dad…

Staying gave her dad the option and opportunity to come home. Maybe not this year, but next year or the year after, he might wake up one morning and realize what he'd thrown away and come home. If he did, she wanted to be here because no matter what he had done, she missed him. He was her dad.

Even as she thought that, an angry voice inside reminded her that he'd kept her in the dark about his troubles and left her behind. When the chips were down, she had without a moment's hesitation taken every cent of her savings and bailed him out. But he hadn't even had the consideration to ask her if she wanted to come with him when he was disappearing for good.

To him, Rayne had been dispensable, just as she had been to her mother.

She took a breath, then rummaged for her key to the newspaper office. The other side of the story could be that her dad might not have involved her because he hadn't wanted her to use her own money to bail him out. But even if he suspected she would use her savings to pay the debt after he was gone, he'd left her his house to replace at least part of it. The house was old and small and definitely in need of remodeling, but selling it would give her the money to return to Baltimore.

Even Jericho had said that her dad signing over the house was proof he wanted to protect her.

Thinking of Jericho made her chest tight. They'd shared something. She knew she hadn't imagined it. But she also knew his family didn't like her. Even if she and Jericho fell madly in love, they'd never marry. There was simply too much past between the two families. It was for the best that she'd insulted him the day before. It got him out of her office and probably out of her life.

Her chest tightened again, but she ignored it. She had enough problems without pining for a man she couldn't have.

Jericho stepped into the borough building to find the crew from the night shift filling out reports and the crew for the day shift pouring coffee into throw-away cups to drink while they drove to the elementary, middle and high schools to make sure everything was okay.

"Good morning."

"Hey, good morning, Chief!" Aaron Jennings said, but his partner, Bill Freedman, didn't look as happy.

Jericho wasn't surprised when Bill followed him into his office. "I heard the rumor that Mark Fegan left town."

"That makes you about three days behind everybody else in Calhoun Corners."

"Was that why Rayne was in the other day?"

Jericho nodded. He should have realized that once his dad had found out about Mark Fegan his officers wouldn't be too far behind. He should have briefed them the day before. But he had been preoccupied with Rayne's troubles, then angry with her for criticizing him rather than thanking him, then worried that he had treated her too harshly. When it came to that woman, he was just a bundle of stupidity, which proved that getting involved with her was nothing but trouble.

"Why don't we go out to the main room and I'll fill you all in as a group."

Bill nodded and led the way. Jericho got everybody's attention and said, "By now you've all heard the rumor that Mark Fegan left town and by now you've probably also guessed that's why Rayne was in the other day."

All four officers nodded.

"She wanted us to help find her dad, but Mark left a note saying he was leaving for personal reasons. At the time, I didn't know if Rayne would make her dad's note public, but by now enough of us know about the situation that it's going to get out one way or another. So it's best that you're all up to speed."

"That's it?" Aaron asked. "He left a note so we don't look for him?"

"The note was very specific about why he was going. He had some personal problems. And his business was failing. Those are two damned good reasons for a man to run. But just to be sure I wasn't ignoring our responsibility, I did a quick check of his office yesterday."

"That's the note you sent to your friend," Martha said.

"I called in a favor and he had a handwriting analyst examine the note to be sure Mark hadn't written it with a gun to his head."

Jericho's four employees nodded and muttered agreements of one sort or another. Even Aaron, who had seemed upset that they weren't investigating, no longer had a problem now that Jericho had explained that he'd done enough preliminary research to prove Mark hadn't met with foul play.

Jericho dismissed them, knowing that Martha and Greg wanted to get home after having worked all night. Bill and Aaron left to patrol. Forgetting about Mark Fegan, Jericho focused on paperwork.

Around ten, he took a turn in the patrol car with Aaron, then went to the diner for lunch with his dad.

"This is becoming something of a daily event," Elaine observed as she set place mats and silverware on the table in front of them.

"Might as well mix business with pleasure," Jericho's dad said with a chuckle.

"So Jericho keeps you informed on what's going on?"

"It's part of my job," Jericho said, getting an odd vibe from the typically chipper hostess. She seemed quietly angry or maybe hostile was a better word. "Mayors are in charge of towns. Chiefs of police technically carry out their wishes to keep the towns safe."

"Right," Elaine said, slamming a setting of silverware rolled in a napkin onto the place mat in front of Jericho's dad. "And does your dad tell you how to do your job?"

"I don't have to tell a guy who's been working in a city like Vegas how to do his job," Ben said.

"No, but I bet you don't mind telling him who he can help and who he can't."

Jericho said, "What?"

"Oh, come on!" Clearly angry now, Elaine glared at Ben then at Jericho. "Rayne's dad has been missing for over two weeks and nobody's lifted a finger—"

"Rayne's dad is not missing," Ben said, but Jericho silenced him with a look.

"Explain exactly what you're talking about," Jericho said, catching Elaine by the wrist and stopping her when it looked as if she intended to drop her angry words and leave.

"Everybody knows Mark is gone."

"Yeah, but you seem to know more details. So spill it."

"What's to spill?" Elaine asked rudely. "You know as well as I do that Mark Fegan is gone. He left poor Rayne with a business that's failing. And you won't do a damned thing to help her."

Jericho could have told Elaine he had done a lot of things to help Rayne find her dad. He could have told her about the travel brochures, old tickets and old itineraries he'd found. He didn't think any of that was Elaine's business.

Instead he rose from his seat. "I'll see you later, Dad."

He left Elaine fuming beside the table, glaring at his dad, and stepped out into the brisk day. Nearly stomping along the cement sidewalk, he strode to the newspaper office. He didn't use the back door. He pushed open the front and stormed up to Rayne's desk.

Bracing both hands on her desk, he leaned into her space. "Wasn't it enough for you to insult me privately yesterday? Did you have to bad-mouth me all over town."

"I didn't bad-mouth you all over town."

"Oh, so you only bad-mouthed me to Elaine?"

"No! I haven't seen Elaine—"

"Right! That's why she all but spat in my face at the diner because I deserted you."

Behind her big glasses, Rayne's blue eyes got round with confusion. "I never said anything—"

Upset with her, but even more tired of being attracted to a woman he shouldn't even like, Jericho pulled away. "She's angry for you. Indignant. No one else could have stirred her up this way but you."

Rayne put her hand on her chest. "I didn't say anything. I've been here all day."

"That doesn't mean you didn't pick up the phone."

"Are you calling me a liar?"

He didn't say anything because he couldn't. Her anger made him want to kiss her. Her eyes were bright. Her skin beautifully flushed. He would have paid a year's salary to kiss her and feel all the passion simmering through her right now.

"Leave."

His breath shivered out of his chest. "I'll leave, but not until we get one thing straight. You're not angry with me. You're angry with your dad. You can't handle that he left you."

"I'm fine."

"Sure. You're great. You're saddled with a business that's failing, begging customers to pay their bills and can't afford to eat."

Her expression sharpened as if he'd slapped her. "You don't know what you're talking about."

"Yeah, like I haven't seen you turn down Elaine's morning pastry."

"So I couldn't afford a Danish. That doesn't mean…"

"You don't buy the Danish you used to buy every morning. You walk to work. Up and down a hill that's difficult in good weather. It's hell in bad. Drew's noticed and commented. My dad's noticed and you can bet your bottom dollar Elaine's noticed."

Rayne said nothing.

"When are you going to get it through your head that this isn't my fault? It isn't my dad's fault. It isn't even your fault. It's your dad's."

Unflinching, Rayne stared at him. "Are you through?"

He rubbed his hand along the back of his neck. "Yeah. Now I'm through."

She pointed at the door and without another word he pivoted and left her.

Jericho Capriotti stormed out of her office and Rayne fell to her desk chair. It was okay that the whole freaking town knew she was in trouble. She couldn't exactly hide that her dad was gone. She also hadn't shrunk from the fact that the paper was in financial trouble. Hell, she'd made it common knowledge that the *Chronicle* wasn't making ends meet when she'd gotten rid of her employees.

But to have the whole town know that she was going hungry was mortifying.

She hadn't told Elaine about Jericho refusing to look for her dad. The humiliation of everyone understanding just how far she had fallen was part of what kept her from seeking comfort in talking out her troubles with a friend. The other part was realizing that no matter how desperate she was, she wouldn't use her bad situation to manipulate public opinion.

But she also knew that her dad wouldn't have hesitated to make Jericho look biased or incapable. And she suddenly saw that Jericho was right. Her dad was a user. He'd had no compunction about leading her down a path to make her believe the town needed rid of Ben Capriotti rather than trusting her with the truth that he'd needed money. Had he trusted her, she would have given him the cash to pay his debt and none of this would be happening.

But he hadn't trusted her because he wasn't always an honest man. Jericho was right in saying he was running from the fact that he'd failed. That he wasn't the big deal he'd always bragged he was. He didn't hesitate to manipulate the truth. He didn't hesitate to manipulate and use people. He hadn't hesitated to use his own daughter.

She had always justified her dad's disparaging Ben Capriotti by telling herself that his desperation drove him to it. But she was desperate and she hadn't folded. She hadn't compromised her morals. She hadn't pushed or manipulated anybody. Yet Jericho thought she had.

Now not only was she forced to deal with the fact that her dad might not have been the guy she wanted him to be, but she also had to deal with the fact that everybody thought she followed in her dad's footsteps. Was a manipulator. Maybe even a liar.

Tears stung her eyes, but instead of giving in to them, she glanced down at the papers on her desk. Accounts to call. Articles to write. Her paper was small and getting smaller. But it was still the voice of the town and it was still the only thing she had. And she wasn't a quitter.

She picked up the unpaid invoice, dialed the number she had scribbled in the margin and went back to work.

That night when Jericho entered his parents' house, he saw that Tia and Drew and Rick and Ashley were also joining him and his parents for dinner. For the first time in ten years the family would be together for a meal and though it seemed like a great phenomenon, Jericho understood why his mother wasn't making a big deal out of it.

At different times after they had become adults, Jericho and Rick had fought with their father and left town. Tia had settled in Pittsburgh after college, but though Jericho's baby sister had gone about leaving in a more subtle way, it was clear to Jericho that Tia hadn't found a job closer to Calhoun Corners for the same reason Rick and Jericho had left. Each wanted the opportunity to make his or her own choices, rather than worry that everything they said or did would somehow reflect on their dad, who constantly rode them to be perfect.

A near fatal heart attack had caused Ben Capriotti to reconsider the way he ran his life. Tia marrying the next-door neighbor, Drew Wallace, a man who had been a family friend, paved the way for an easy transition for Tia to reenter her parents' lives as a mature adult. Coming home with the degree he'd avoided like the plague, getting a job on the most renowned horse farm in Calhoun Corners, proving himself to be a good father and settling down with Ashley Meljac had eased Rick into the family again. Then, without fanfare, their father had offered Jericho a job and, without fanfare, he had accepted. The family had been eased together, no excuses, no finger pointing, no blaming about the past. And that was the way Jericho knew it should be.

"What the hell was Elaine talking about today?"

Brought out of his thoughts by his dad's question, Jericho took a breath. "The same thing you and I discussed the other day. Except she has the other opinion. You think I should stay away from involvement in Mark

Fegan leaving town. Elaine thinks I should be involved. You heard the discussion."

Ben blew his breath out on a sigh. "How do things like this get so blown out of proportion?"

Drew laughed as he took the bowl of mashed potatoes pregnant Tia handed to him. "Are you kidding, Ben? Nothing stays a secret in a town the size of Calhoun Corners."

The truth of that gave Jericho an odd feeling.

Holding Rick's sleeping infant daughter, Ashley laughed. Jericho noticed how Rick's eyes seemed to caress his beautiful blond fiancée as she spoke. "I can testify to that. People on the street knew my dad was retiring two weeks before I did."

Ben took a breath. "Okay. People in small towns gossip. But this wasn't something that would normally get out."

Rick, Ashley, Tia and Drew laughed. Jericho's mother sighed. "Eat your dinner, Ben. There's no way we'll figure out how Elaine knew Jericho wasn't going to investigate."

Jericho's gaze shot to his mother. "How do *you* know?" Just as quickly, he looked at his dad. "Did you tell her?"

Ben shook his head, at the same time that Elizabeth said, "Janie Alberter told me."

"The woman in the dress shop?" Jericho asked skeptically.

"She's the one who told me," Ashley said.

"And who told her?"

Rick laughed. "Come on, Jericho. How are we supposed to know that?"

But Ashley said, "She told me Olivia Richmond told her."

Jericho frowned. "Olivia Richmond? The old school-teacher? How would she know?"

Ashley shrugged. "Maybe Rayne told her."

Elizabeth shook her head. "What's to tell? Rayne is running the paper on her own. She laid off her staff. That means she's in financial trouble. Her dad is gone, but Jericho didn't launch an investigation. I don't think there is an origin. I think what happened was simple deductive reasoning."

"You mean the gossip that got back to Elaine might have been nothing but a few people guessing?"

The six adults at the table all looked at Jericho.

Finally his mother said, "That's what gossip is, Jericho. Enough speculation that somebody comes up with a plausible story. Is it true?"

"That I won't help her?" Jericho asked.

Elizabeth nodded.

"Yes and no. I did a short, private investigation and came up empty."

"So why don't you just tell people that?"

He sighed. "I did tell my officers."

"Why don't you keep investigating?" Ashley asked.

"Mark left a note. Technically, he isn't missing. Once I verified that he traveled a lot and had a handwriting analyst say that in his opinion the note hadn't been written under any strain, I believed I had proven that he left of his own volition, which isn't a crime."

But it wasn't entirely fair, either. Not because Jericho wanted to take away Mark's right to run from his failure, but because Mark had left behind a daughter who was struggling, suffering, *starving* for his mistakes.

And Jericho had just read her the riot act.

He waited until his brother and sister and their families had gone, and his parents had turned in for the night, before putting on his jacket and boots and trudging out into the night again. It was nearly midnight, but Jericho knew that Rayne could still be working. If she wasn't, she would be at her house. Hopefully she wasn't yet in bed.

He drove to town, passing the newspaper office because it was dark. At least she wasn't working into the wee hours of the night. He swung his truck onto Prospect Avenue and drove to the top, then down her street. A light was on.

He took a breath, parked the truck, walked up to her front door and knocked.

She answered the door in sloppy sweatpants and a T-shirt with no makeup. But also with no glasses and her blond hair flowing around her. Jericho swallowed.

"What?"

Luckily, her attitude was still the same. "I wanted to apologize."

"Let's see? What could you have to apologize for? Deserting me? Refusing to help me? Chitchatting with your staff about my problems? Or yelling at me? The list is so long and varied I'm not quite sure what you mean."

He sighed. "I wasn't chitchatting with my staff. I had to brief them." He raked his fingers through his short hair, spiking it. "Look, we got off on the wrong foot for a hundred and ten different reasons." Half of them had to do with the fact that he wanted to sleep with the fantasy Rayne he created, but he sure as hell couldn't tell her that. "But the only real reason for me to apologize to you is for accusing you of complaining to Elaine. I should have believed you when you said you hadn't."

The porch light of the house next door suddenly lit. Rayne noticed it and opened the door a little wider, indicating he should enter. He agreed completely. The last thing either of them needed was to be seen together at her house late at night. Or the next thing they'd know the rumor would be circulating that they were sleeping together.

He walked into her small, cramped foyer and she motioned for him to follow her into her living room. Old furniture was piled high with magazines and newspapers. Every available space held a book, clipping or printout.

"It's a mess, isn't it?"

Jericho shrugged. "It's a man's house."

"It's the house of a man who refused to throw anything away."

"Yet another reason he just chucked everything and ran."

She nodded.

"That's why I can't look for him, Rayne. With one quick peek into his life anybody can see a hundred reasons he'd want to leave. Though his creditors aren't too happy, he has the right to go. And for all we know, he could be paying his debts."

"Or he could be alone, living on other credit cards, running."

"I'm sorry. But that's his choice."

She nodded, but Jericho could see from the expression in her pretty eyes what she was thinking. Her dad might have had the right and reason to go, but he'd left her to clean up his mess—literally.

"You know, you could sell this house and pay off your dad's bills and walk away. Or you could just pay off the debts secured by this property and keep the rest of the money. Or you could rent the house and go back to Baltimore."

"Wow. You sure seem to be in a hurry for me to go."

He shook his head in protest. "I'm not." But he was. Every time he looked at her, he saw her as another person. Worse, when she spoke civilly, as she was right now, he felt as if he could see that other person inside her, struggling to get out. And that was not only stupid, it was none of his concern. Yet part of him wanted—no part of him longed—to free her.

And that was the most ridiculous thing of all.

"I'm pointing out your options as a way to help you."

She laughed and combed her fingers through her hair, calling his attention to it, reminding him it wasn't just long, it was also thick. Thick and probably silky.

He swallowed.

"The next thing you know, you'll be volunteering to help me clean it out so I can rent it."

"You could get a renter to clear it out himself by offering to give him the first month's rent free."

She gasped. "You *are* trying to get rid of me!"

"I'm trying to help you! Can't you just accept it?"

"No! Not help from you, anyway! Your family hates mine, Jericho."

When she used his name, Jericho's chest tightened and his nerves sprang to life. Never before had his name sounded so intimate. So personal. So sensual.

"I won't be run out of town."

"I'm not running you out of town."

"Right! What other reason could you possibly have for wanting me to go."

Knowing she wouldn't believe him if he put this into words, Jericho grabbed her shoulders, yanked her to him and kissed her.

He kissed her deeply, instantly falling into the act as if he were made to kiss her. He devoured her mouth, tasting her, enjoying her, and she responded. As if she were made to kiss him.

That realization was the one that penetrated the haze being created by the sheer pleasure of kissing her. He could easily tag and accept what he felt for her as lust. When she got involved, things weren't so simple any more. He didn't want to hurt her. He also didn't want to like her. He most certainly wouldn't get involved in a relationship with a woman from Calhoun Corners that was only sexual. People in his little town didn't date for fun. They courted. Anybody seeing anybody else was doing so with the intention of deciding if they were right for marriage. That was just the way small towns were. If you didn't want to marry somebody you didn't date her. Since he didn't want to marry anybody, he couldn't date *anybody*. At least not anybody in town.

He pulled away and she blinked at him. For all he knew, she had been surprised by the kiss and would be angry.

Hell, she *should* be angry.

"Sorry."

She gaped at him. "Sorry? What kind of comment is that?"

"It's the kind of comment that says I shouldn't have kissed you," he shot back. "For Pete's sake! We're oil and water. I don't want to be involved with you."

She stretched to a nearby table and grabbed her

glasses, then shoved them on. With the lenses that allowed her to see clearly, she studied his face, spending a long time looking into his eyes. Finally she smiled.

"You're *really* attracted to me."

"Big deal. You're a pretty girl."

"No, I'm not!" she said, then she laughed. "I mean, I know that if I spend time at the beauty parlor and put on makeup I can be as attractive as the next girl—"

Jericho couldn't help his expression of disbelief. *As attractive as the next girl?* Wow, she had no idea.

"But, right now, dressed like this," she said, grabbing a handful of her pant leg and stretching it to illustrate its complete formlessness, "I'm not even average. I'm waaaay below average."

"All right." Being attracted to the town ugly duckling made him sound either slightly nuts or like a guy looking to take advantage of her vulnerability. He wasn't either of those, but he wasn't going to get out of this without an explanation. "All this can be cleared up if I make a simple admission."

She raised one eyebrow in question.

"I saw you once."

"You saw me?"

"At a party in Baltimore. You were all dressed up. And I thought you looked really good." He took a breath. "Men are pigs. I saw you looking great and it caused all kinds of questions to enter my head. Including things like what kissing you would be like. Now I know."

She tilted her head in question, then said, "Yeah, now you know."

But there was an odd quality to her voice. It wasn't disbelief. Disbelief he could have handled. He would have *liked* disbelief. Then he could feel they were kindred spirits. Instead, the tone of her voice was more of a curiosity, as if she found his attraction to her interesting. And that was just plain wrong.

"So now we can both get on with the rest of our lives." Her expression changed and he quickly added, "Not that I'm trying to get you to leave town. You can stay. You can go. In fact, that's what I'm going to do right now. Go."

Chapter Five

Dumbstruck, Rayne watched Jericho leave her house. She was shocked that he'd seen her in Baltimore. Everybody thought he hadn't been anywhere near Calhoun Corners after he moved west, but obviously he had visited friends here on the East Coast. When she'd lived in Baltimore she'd had a totally different life. She'd gone to lots of parties, worn bright, sometimes revealing clothes, had an expense account, lived with a man.

She drew a long breath. A man who had ultimately hurt her. And Jericho Capriotti would hurt her, too. Except…

She needed to know if her dad really had been protecting her rather than deserting her, when he'd left Calhoun Corners. She didn't want to carry around the empty, lonely feeling of being abandoned if it wasn't true. But if he had deserted her, she needed to move on.

But she couldn't do either until she knew the truth and she wouldn't know the truth until she found her dad.

And she couldn't find her dad without help. Rayne was smart enough to figure out that when Jericho said searching for her dad would be a long process, he was also saying the process would be even longer if she hired less than the best private investigator. So she needed the best, somebody like his skip tracer friend.

But when she'd told Mac she couldn't pay his fee up front, he'd been agreeable to a payment plan as long as she passed a credit check. But she hadn't passed the credit check because technically she didn't have an income. At least not as long as she stayed at the *Chronicle.*

But if Jericho vouched for her, saying that she was good for the money, his friend might go to work on the promise of being paid later.

But Jericho wouldn't vouch for her if they weren't friends. Or something.

The "or something" made her swallow. It wasn't her intention to sleep with Jericho Capriotti, but his kissing her proved that he felt something for her and a little flirting might inspire him to put in a good word for her with his friend. She wasn't worried that their flirtation would go any further than that. From the way he'd run out of her house after kissing her, it was clear he didn't want to follow through on the attraction he felt for her. His family didn't like her and he wouldn't want to upset them. She couldn't blame him for that. But she and Jericho could indulge in a private flirtation and he could even do her a private favor without anyone in the Capriotti clan discovering.

Her reasoning made so much sense she ran up the steps and down the short hall to her bedroom. She ripped open the closet door and rummaged past her few normal clothes—the bland, oversize T-shirts and jeans she wore now—until she got to the things in the back.

At the sudden sight of so much color she caught her breath, remembering how she had behaved, the person she had been wearing those clothes. She couldn't believe she was considering turning into that other person again. But if she wanted to find out the truth, she had to be willing to do this.

She reached for a pretty peacock-blue suit.

The next morning Jericho walked into the borough building with a splitting headache. He hadn't slept much the night before. He'd kept going over that kiss and the reasons for it until eventually he realized both he and Rayne were victims of emotional overwhelm. Since the end result of his tossing and turning the night before was that he had absolved himself of any guilt for kissing Rayne, Jericho was fine with a little headache.

After handling his typical morning routine, he rode with Martha for the school patrol. When he returned to the borough building, he found his brother Rick sitting on the corner of Greg's desk entertaining him with stories about his daughter Ruthie.

"What's up?" he asked, walking up the aisle between the four desks.

Rick rose. "Nothing. Ashley took Ruthie shopping and I thought I'd check on you."

Jericho laughed. "You? Check on *me?*"

"Hey, I'm the settled one now. Officially the family good child."

"Tia's officially the family good child. Always has been. Always will be."

"Okay, then I'm officially the family good *boy*."

"Mom sent you, didn't she?"

Rick grimaced. "Yes. She says you do nothing but work and she's worried."

Jericho laughed. "Wow. How times have changed."

"I know," Rick agreed. "They used to wonder if we'd ever be able to hold down a job. Now Mom's worried that you work too much." He slapped Jericho on the back. "So, let's have a late breakfast together, then I can go to Mom's and at least tell her you stop for meals."

Jericho glanced at his watch. Nine o'clock. The breakfast rush would be over at the diner, and he hadn't yet eaten. A break for food wasn't such a bad idea. "You buying?"

Rich shrugged. "I guess it's the least I can do for a poorly paid public servant."

"My thought exactly." He turned to Greg. "I'll be back in an hour."

"Right, Chief."

They walked out into the warm November day and Rick said, "Does that bother you?"

"What?"

"That everybody calls you Chief?"

"I'm getting accustomed to it," Jericho said, stepping to the side to let Emma Jean Johnson pass.

"Morning, Chief," she said, and Rick laughed.

"I guess you have to get accustomed to it or spend the rest of your life here angry."

"There's nothing wrong with being a little angry," Jericho said, pushing open the diner door. "Keeps a guy on his toes."

"Also keeps a guy broke and in jail."

When Jericho opened his mouth to rebut his statement,

Rick held up a hand. "You've been to jail. We've both spent a night or two in jail for fighting. Don't deny it."

"I can't deny it," Jericho said as Elaine motioned for them to seat themselves since the diner was now fairly empty. "I can't deny that I'm reformed. But I'm also not going to turn into a sap."

"A sap?"

"You know," Jericho said, sliding onto the bench seat of the booth. "One of those guys who thinks growing up means he has to be nice to everybody."

"You wouldn't by any chance be throwing slings and arrows my way?"

Jericho's brow furrowed and he stared at Rick. "For what?"

"Are you backhandedly telling me I got soft just because I stopped getting arrested for bar fights?"

"No," Jericho said, then he laughed. "Actually, Rick, it seems to me you've got the world by a string. You found somebody and you also found your calling. You didn't let the gossip push you around, or your past dictate who you have to be. And you didn't have to strap on a badge to prove anything."

"Do you think you did?"

Jericho glanced around the nearly empty diner. "I don't know."

"Do you think people would like you less if you weren't the chief of police?"

"No. I think coming back as a respected member of law enforcement has made it easy for people to accept me. Now, I want to keep their respect."

Rick shrugged. "Nothing wrong with that."

Elaine came over and took their order. She didn't

seem angry today, and Jericho assumed he'd been forgiven. After she left, the conversation shifted to Rick's plans for Seven Hills and Jericho felt a wave of respect for his brother. Only Rick could fall in love with a debutante, be deeded half of a multimillion-dollar business as an engagement present and not give a damn what anybody thought. He loved Ashley. He intended to make a life with her. He no longer felt the need to prove himself.

Jericho didn't exactly believe he had to prove himself, but he didn't want anybody confusing him with the troublemaker he had been in the past. At the same time, he couldn't let anybody think that straightening out his life had weakened him. If anything, he wanted them to realize that the straight and narrow path he'd chosen had made him stronger.

After they ate, Elaine brought their check and Rick grabbed it. Jericho tried to take it from him. "I was kidding when I said breakfast was on you."

"I know. But I wasn't kidding when I said I was paying. So finish your coffee and let's get going."

Knowing there was no point arguing with his pig-headed brother, Jericho picked up his white mug to drain the last of his coffee, glancing over at the diner door as it opened. Rayne entered. When he saw her bright blue suit, with a skirt that ended far enough above to knee to remind him that she had great legs, his mug stopped halfway to his mouth.

Rick said, "What?" then turned and followed the direction of Jericho's gaze. When he saw Rayne, he burst out laughing. "I'll be damned."

"Shut up, Rick!"

"What?" Rick said, giving Jericho a curious look before angling his body to get another peek at Rayne. As she walked to the counter, Rick studied her enough that Jericho felt like reaching across the table and forcing him to turn around.

"Aren't you engaged?"

"I'm not looking because I'm interested. I'm looking because I'm confused. What the hell has gotten into her?"

At the complete lack of attraction in Rick's voice, Jericho relaxed. "Her dad left her with a business that's failing. I think she has a right to be a little confused."

"She doesn't look confused to me. She looks very comfortable in that…that…"

"Color?" Jericho asked pointedly, and Rick again hooted with laughter.

"You *like* her!"

"No, I do not like her. I feel sorry for her. And believe me I have reason, which I am not going to tell you."

"Don't want to be part of the gossip mill?"

Jericho shook his head. "No. Don't want to break a confidence."

"A confidence." Rick whistled. "Wow. A confidence with a Fegan. That's gotta be against one of Dad's rules."

"It's more of a chief-of-police confidence than a Capriotti confidence. So stop. And stop staring."

Rick turned from staring at Rayne and grinned at his brother.

"Grow up, Rick."

Rick shook his head. "Are you nuts? I'm teasing you."

"Whatever."

"Boy, either you really like this woman or you're

more sensitive about coming home to your hell-raising roots than I thought."

"I'm not interested."

He might be physically attracted to Rayne, but he didn't *like* her. As if to prove it, he rose from the booth and walked to the counter.

"My brother's paying," he told Elaine before he casually turned to Rayne, if only to show his damned brother that he could be in the same room with a pretty female without being overwhelmed with lust like a randy teenager.

But when she smiled up at him, his breath stuttered. Lord, she was beautiful. Her contacts didn't diminish the bright color of her blue eyes the way the thick lenses of her glasses did. Without the distraction of her glasses it was also easy to see her flawless complexion. Add that to the way her yellow hair tumbled to her shoulders and the way the color of the suit just made her look pretty, and Jericho fell speechless.

Rick nudged him in the back. "Yeah, I'm paying because I'm not so sure my brother can figure out the tip right now."

He said it as if he were teasing, but Jericho knew that Rick was right and it infuriated him. He was behaving like an idiot. And it had to stop.

He said, "Good morning, Rayne," then turned and slapped Rick on the back. "I'll see you later. Thanks for breakfast."

He walked out into the sunny November morning without another word. He wasn't mad at Rick for teasing him. Teasing was what brothers did. He wasn't angry with Rayne for dressing up. If he were the suspicious type, he would think that now that she knew he found her attractive she was taunting him. But he wasn't a sixteen-year-old. He didn't believe the whole world revolved around him or his sex life. He knew Rayne had personal problems. He knew she was confused. And as a mature, intelligent man with a town to protect, he was taking the logical route and deciding she'd worn something pretty to cheer herself up. End of story.

When Jericho and Rick left the diner, Elaine handed Rayne her cup of coffee. "Here you are, sweetie."

Striving to be casual, Rayne paid for the coffee with coins she found in a cup behind some things in the pantry and casually said, "No comment about my suit?"

Elaine tilted her head, studying Rayne. "That color is very good on you."

"Nothing else?"

Elaine smiled. "Honey, I know you're upset. I know your daddy left you with bills. I even suspect that when you come in here you'd like to buy the Danish you used to get every morning, but you don't have the money."

When Rayne went to protest, Elaine stopped her. "You don't have to admit or deny anything. I know the whole town thinks I'm a gossip—and I guess I am—but there are some things I consider sacred. A woman struggling to get past something she didn't bring on herself is one of them."

"Thanks."

"So, I understand the dressing up. You're keeping up your spirits. Or maybe you're trying to impress a new advertiser. Whatever it is, honey, I'm behind you."

Rayne smiled, pleased that Elaine had picked an explanation for her fancy clothes that made complete sense—even if it was wrong—because that was the tale Elaine would spread and most people would believe it.

"And if I thought you'd take the Danish, I'd give you one."

Rayne shook her head. "Can't do that."

"Well, if the day comes when you think you could take the Danish," Elaine said, squeezing Rayne's arm, "you let me know."

"Okay."

Rayne left the diner and began the walk to her office almost cheering for joy. Not only did she have Elaine in her corner, but she hadn't missed the way Jericho's mouth had fallen open when he'd seen her. She had absolutely no idea what she was doing. Back in Baltimore, she'd been dressing for a specific man. He'd been calling the shots, virtually telling her what to do. She didn't have a coach here, but she was a smart woman, and from Jericho's reaction she had more than a sneaking suspicion she wasn't doing so badly by simply winging it.

Rayne didn't merely consider it a lucky break when she received two checks in Friday's mail; Monday morning when she was able to withdraw cash without a hassle, she decided it was a sign. It bothered her that Jericho realized how broke she was. Given time to think through the situation, she recognized his bringing her food was another clue that he had a soft spot for her, but she also didn't want him thinking she was weak. She didn't want to get his help out of weakness. Eventually she would have money to pay his friend. And that was the real bottom line. She wasn't asking for charity. She was asking for deferred payments. So tonight, she would show Jericho she didn't need charity. Then, when she asked him to ask his friend to help her, he'd be confident she was good for the money.

Knowing that Jericho gave everybody Monday evening off because everyone worked extra shifts on the weekend, and would be in the borough building alone, Rayne made her plan.

Late that afternoon she had bought two sandwiches from Elaine, packed a picnic basket, and put on a pair of tight jeans with a torso-caressing blue lace top. She covered them with her big wool coat, but that wasn't because she didn't have a prettier coat. It was a strategy.

Entering the silent borough building, she saw the four gray metal desks that created a square of sorts in the center of the large main room. Bright overhead lights exaggerated the fact that all four were empty. The scent of overbrewed coffee wafted from the coffeemaker on the window ledge.

"Anybody here?" she called, feeling foolish. She knew Jericho gave his team Monday night off, but couldn't believe he would leave the borough building unlocked when he was out on patrol. She gingerly made her way to the back office, just as he walked through the door.

"Rayne?"

"Hey," she said, so nervous she was surprised her voice didn't shiver. She held up the picnic basket. "I brought you supper since you brought me lunch last week." She shrugged. "Turnabout is fair play."

She hadn't missed the fact that Jericho had taken a quick inventory of her face before his gaze had stalled on her hair, which she had curled but otherwise left in sexy disarray.

Knowing there was no time like the present, she set her basket on one of the desks and slipped off her coat, then watched his gaze fall to her bright blue U-necked top then tight, low-rise jeans.

He cleared his throat. "What did you bring?"

Thankful that he wasn't going to make this difficult by asking for an explanation, she smiled. "I'm not very creative. Since I knew you liked roast beef, I had Elaine make the same sandwiches you brought me the other day." Honesty and gratitude collided in her chest and forced her to add, "And I wanted to thank you again."

He caught her gaze. "You didn't have to."

She shrugged. "I pay my debts."

"It wasn't a debt."

"Okay, then, how about if we say that I just like to return favors?"

Enough time passed that Rayne thought he would refuse her. But he took a breath and shrugged. "I am hungry."

"Good." Deciding to move as quickly as possible before he changed his mind, Rayne picked up the basket again. "Is there an empty desk we can use out here, or do you want to go into your office?"

"I don't like to use anybody else's desk for anything. I like my people to have a sense of privacy and place." He motioned to his office behind him. "So let's go back here."

She nodded and walked toward him, realizing that in his usual gentlemanly way he was waiting for her to precede him. But the minute she passed him she also realized that her short top provided him with a very clear view of her backside, and her face flared with color.

Jericho had never been more confused in his life. He understood Rayne wanting to pay him back for the food he had brought to her. He also understood that she would come right out and say it. Pride was something he knew well and he was comfortable dealing with it. What he didn't understand was her change of dress, except that it was mighty suspicious that she dressed as the woman he remembered right after he told her he had seen her in Baltimore, admitted he'd found her attractive and kissed her.

For that reason he darned near took the sandwich and sent her packing. But understanding her pride, he couldn't do that. Her dad had left her alone with a failing business and a bushel of debt and she needed to show everybody she was strong.

He caught a glimpse of her bottom as she walked into his office and because he was behind her he lifted his eyes to the heavens. Being in the same room with her dressed like his fantasy girl was not going to be easy, and he genuinely wished he wasn't so understanding. But he wasn't in emotional overload tonight. He didn't have to worry that his base instincts would get the better of him. He didn't have to worry that he'd have to kiss her to prove a point. Things would be fine.

"I'm surprised you're not hard at work." That was the first thing that had come to his mind and also a topic he felt safe discussing.

"The paper has to be at the printer first thing Monday

morning," she said, setting her picnic basket on his desk. "Technically this is my only night off."

"Right." Jericho glanced around the room, feeling awkward, but also recognizing that taking the time to be nice to her was a good thing for both of them. They might not ever be able to be real friends, but they didn't have to be enemies, either.

Rayne pulled a thermos from the basket. "I hope you like cocoa."

"Cocoa," he said, shaking his head, surprised because he considered cocoa a drink for kids. "I haven't had cocoa in years."

"Then I've got perfect timing," she said, taking two mugs from the basket.

With nothing to do but watch her, Jericho could see that her hands were small and tonight her fingernails were painted a pretty pale pink. Tonight, everything about her looked soft and feminine, and he felt himself slipping again, but he saw the small can of cocoa she pulled from the basket and he laughed.

"You use real cocoa," he said, amazed.

She turned and smiled. "The stuff that you make by adding hot water is good in a pinch but I like real cocoa."

Jericho stared at her, his heart pumping. He could swear she was flirting with him and, without warning, he was back at the party, looking at the girl in the tight red dress, remembering how she smiled, how she laughed, how she flirted.

The room became unbearably warm. Rayne might claim that woman wasn't the real her, but either she had only been kidding herself or his imagination was pretty damned good. To him she seemed perfectly at home in these clothes, making cocoa and casual conversation, and he suddenly realized it wasn't wise for him to be so close to her no matter how good his intentions.

He glanced at the door. "You know what? Maybe I should just save the sandwich for later."

"Why?" she asked, laughing, continuing to sound like the woman at the party, and everything inside Jericho responded. He wanted to know her. He wanted to laugh with her. He wanted to figure out why this Rayne could be happy and the other one couldn't be anything but serious.

She smiled prettily. "Our families aren't exactly friends, but nobody has to know that we eat sandwiches together."

Desperate to keep his perspective, he reminded himself that his dad had been recovering from a heart attack when her dad had raked him over hot coals in the paper.

"Nobody needs to told, but somebody always finds out."

She walked over to him and smiled up at him. "Afraid?"

Jericho could smell her soft, floral scent and his brain froze.

"There's something between us and though you're probably right, we can't pursue that, we can at least be friends."

"I'm just supposed to forget what your dad did to mine?"

"You read my dad's note. He was trapped. He thought he had no choice but to make the only deal being offered."

Jericho hadn't forgotten or downplayed that part of the note. He had considered it sleazy and manipulative that Mark had used the newspaper to undermine his dad's bid for reelection as a way to save himself. But though he could picture Mark Fegan cheating, and he could even picture teenage Rayne, the adolescent who adored her dad, following his every order, he couldn't picture this Rayne, the one who was soft-spoken, intelligent and educated, manipulating the truth or using the newspaper for personal gain. And that was really why he couldn't easily turn her away. Those actions didn't fit with the woman he'd seen in Baltimore any more than they fit the smart, determined Rayne he'd seen glimpses of since her father's disappearance. Reminding himself of her part in things didn't diminish his attraction because it didn't make sense. This Rayne wouldn't be so easily taken in my her dad and Jericho needed to understand why she had helped him.

"So why did *you* want Auggie Malloy in?"

"I didn't. But when I came back from Baltimore, I was devastated and I didn't have the mental energy to think through the things my dad was asking me to research." She caught his gaze and Jericho had to fight not to swallow hard. She was so beautiful.

"Your father had also had his heart attack. He was sick and because I was vulnerable it wasn't difficult for my dad to convince me that it was time for new leadership, if only because your dad wasn't healthy enough to be mayor anymore." She looked down as if ashamed, but returned her gaze to his before she added, "It wasn't my job to question my dad. He was my boss. I was an employee. And your dad was sick. Maybe too sick to run an entire town."

Jericho swallowed. It seemed that every time she

held his gaze for more than three seconds he saw the woman he perceived to be the real Rayne, and he simply wanted to enjoy her. But even with her part in the election explained, there were a million other reasons not to pursue their attraction.

First, Rayne was the same age as his baby sister, which made her too much younger than he was. Second, her dad's name wasn't a good word in his parents' household. Third, she didn't believe she was the girl he kept seeing. She'd even told him she didn't want to be that girl. Fourth, he did not want another relationship. Living with Laura Beth had turned him into somebody who couldn't handle a simple breakup without spending two years in a bottle. He didn't want to go back to being that person. He was chief of police in this town. He had to be strong.

He took a step back, away from her. "I've got to make a patrol." He nodded in the direction of his desk, said, "Thanks for the sandwich," then turned and walked out of his office.

Chapter Six

Pain exploded through Rayne when Jericho walked away from his office, and she knew why. She might have fooled herself into thinking this picnic had only been a way to befriend him to get his help. She might have really only intended it that way. But she'd had a crush on Jericho Capriotti forever. In the past few days he'd shown her a mature, responsible side that was nearly irresistible and she'd been falling for him again.

Not only was that wrong, but being head over heels crazy about him made her plan to befriend him to get his help impossible. She couldn't ever be friends with this guy. There was simply too much history and too much attraction between them.

Repacking her picnic, she resigned herself to the fact that she wouldn't be able to "persuade" Jericho to help her. But she had his skip tracer friend's phone number. She also knew his price. Saving until she could afford to pay the tracer up front was far less humbling than trying to befriend a man who didn't want to have to be nice to her. No matter how difficult it was not knowing her father's status, she could wait the time it would take to save enough money.

Humiliated by Jericho's rejection, Rayne wouldn't have dressed in her former clothes again the next morning, but Elaine believed Rayne was wearing bright outfits to cheer herself up. If she went back to jeans and oversize T-shirts, Elaine would ask why and Rayne didn't think she could come up with something creative enough to explain it away.

So, after her shower Tuesday morning, she put on a raspberry-colored sweater and low-riding jeans, fluffed out her hair and even put in her contacts. To her surprise, she didn't feel foolish walking down the street to the post office and then to the diner. The only people who stopped and stared were men, so she knew the women had grown accustomed to seeing her dressed a little better and the men would soon follow suit.

But the reaction of the men also told her she looked pretty damned good, and that lifted her spirits. Jericho Capriotti didn't want her, but she wasn't a complete washout as a woman. She straightened her shoulders and fluffed out her hair a bit before walking into the diner.

"I'll have that Danish today," she called to Elaine who turned from the counter with a laugh.

"Not worried about your figure anymore?" Elaine teased, her eyes twinkling with amusement.

"With so many men watching it lately, I don't think I have to."

Elaine shook her head and chuckled as she wrapped

a cherry Danish in waxed paper and slid it into a brown bag. "Coffee?"

"Yes. Thank you."

"You sound very chipper today."

"I am chipper," she said, just as the diner door opened. To keep her next comment private, she leaned forward and whispered, "I got a few more checks in this morning's mail."

"Oh, Rayne! That's great," Elaine said, setting Rayne's coffee on the counter so she could take her money. Reaching for the button on the cash register, Elaine said, "Good morning, Jericho."

Because her back was to him, Rayne squeezed her eyes shut. She'd made a complete fool of herself the night before and the disgrace of that was enough to keep her hiding in her office for weeks. But she knew hiding would only make matters worse. Jericho didn't want her and she shouldn't want him. It wasn't the first time they've been through this, but it would be the last. She had gotten the "no thanks" message the night before, and she respected it. Now, it was time to move on.

With a quick breath for courage, she turned with a smile. "Good morning, Chief."

Already on his way to a booth, he stopped and faced her, and though Rayne didn't want to react, her breath quivered. He looked so goshed darned sexy in his uniform, but more than that, she now knew there was more to him than a handsome face, piercing eyes and broad shoulders. In the past week, she had learned he was kind, had compassion, and was a man of substance. Integrity.

Which was exactly why he hadn't wanted anything to do with her the night before. He wouldn't indulge in a flirtation. He wasn't a fake or a phony. He was everything a smart woman looked for in a man, and she couldn't have him.

He quietly said, "Good morning, Rayne," and though his greeting was perfectly normal, something in his voice caught Rayne's attention and her gaze jumped to his. She could have handled a bit of regret in his voice or his eyes, if only because of her sweater. Instead, she saw longing. The same feelings currently tightening her chest and making her breath quiver were in his eyes. He *did* want her. Maybe not as much as she wanted him, but he wanted her. Yet they had to walk away.

He didn't say anything else, only turned and strode back to the booth in the far corner. She watched him for a few seconds more and when she turned it was to find Elaine staring at her.

"That's kind of like reaching for the stars, don't you think?"

Rayne swallowed. "Yeah."

"Especially after what your daddy did to his daddy."

Rayne smiled slightly and nodded. She said, "Yeah," again, then quickly made her way out of the diner, not about to get into a full-scale discussion about this because there was no "this."

But she couldn't stop thinking about her dad and Jericho's dad and her own part in things. She tried to tell herself that Jericho ignoring the attraction between them was the equivalent to her siding with her dad during the election, but now that she knew the real reason her father had wanted Ben Capriotti out of office, the excuse rang hollow. The two things were nothing alike. The real problem had been that Rayne had come home devastated and vulnerable, and if she took her thoughts to their logical conclusion she'd also have to admit that her dad might have taken advantage of her.

She acknowledged the possibility, but she also told herself that her father was in dire straits. He might have taken advantage of her vulnerability but it was because he wasn't thinking clearly, either.

She spent the afternoon trying to put it out of her mind, but the thought that her dad had taken advantage of her crept into her brain every few seconds. On the heels of that she remembered the look of longing in Jericho's eyes and the way he could nonetheless turn away, and she experienced a pain so sharp it stole her breath. Could it be that she had lost the love of her life because she'd trusted her father?

Rayne had thought she was at the lowest point of her life when she was so broke she couldn't afford food, but she suddenly realized that recognizing her dad might have used her beat out going hungry as her lowest point. She'd come home depressed from the biggest rejection of her life and the one person she trusted beyond all others had used her. Deliberately. For his own gain. Not caring that his using her might have consequences for her.

At seven o'clock that night she couldn't take her internal despondency anymore. She rose from her desk at the *Chronicle* office and walked to her house, where she took her car keys from the holder by the back door and headed out of town. At the Capriotti's horse farm, she didn't hesitate. She got out of her car, jogged up the porch steps and knocked on the door.

Elizabeth, Jericho's mother, answered. "I'm sorry to

bother you, Mrs. Capriotti, but is your husband home by any chance?"

Jericho's mother didn't instantly answer. She took a few seconds to study Rayne and Rayne stood still under her scrutiny. Finally, she smiled and lightly said, "This isn't business, isn't it? Because my husband's off duty for the day."

Though her voice was light and cheerful, Elizabeth was clearly protecting her husband. Rayne didn't blame her. "It's more personal."

"Not an interview?"

Rayne shook her head. "No, ma'am."

"Okay, then, I'll get him." She turned and walked back the corridor to the right, disappearing through what appeared to be the last door at the end of the hall. After a minute she stepped out of the room and said, "Come on back, please."

Rayne took a breath and strode down the hall and into the room, which was an office or den. Ben Capriotti rose from a well-used but obviously expensive, brown leather sofa and Rayne nearly froze. This was another difference between her family and Jericho's. Her family was poor and his was rich, and she didn't know how or why she'd forgotten.

Ben pointed at a chair that matched the sofa. "Have a seat."

"Uh, no. Thanks, though. I just came because I wanted to…" She took a breath. "There's no easy way to say this. So I'm just going to come right out and apologize for what my dad and I did to you in the last election."

To her surprise, Ben burst out laughing. "Apologize?" He screwed up his face in exaggerated confusion. "To a Capriotti."

Rayne took another long breath. "Yes."

"May I ask why?"

"I know the rumors are around town that my dad owed money."

"To a loan shark," Ben supplied. "The other half of that rumor is that he couldn't pay it back so he agreed to do everything in his power to get Auggie Malloy elected."

"Yes."

"But he failed."

"Yes," Rayne agreed. Knowing she couldn't speak for her dad, but wanting to right her part of things, she said, "I'm here because I want you to understand that I think what we did was wrong."

"Not selling any papers?" Ben asked sarcastically.

"Or ads." Rayne shook her head. "But that's not why I'm here. I've decided to give up the paper," she said, only that second realizing it was true. Why would she want to keep it? Her dad had made a mess of their reputation in Calhoun Corners, but he'd also fixed it so that she could walk away. He hadn't contacted her in weeks. He'd deserted her. And she could have a job in Baltimore or Washington or Chicago with less strain, less stress and a real paycheck. "So I'm not apologizing to make my life easier. I'm just apologizing."

"And I should accept your apology just like that?"

"I came home from Baltimore crushed because the man I had been living with left me. I wasn't myself. Had I been, I would have seen that my dad was going too far.

I would have pushed him to tell me why, and I wouldn't have taken any part in the election stuff."

"Your boyfriend had left you?"

Elizabeth's question surprised Rayne so much she turned to face her. "Yes. And I know that's not much of an excuse—"

"Were you together long?"

"Since college."

"Seven years?"

"Six."

"And he just left?"

Tired, defeated, Rayne shrugged. "Yes, and I was absolutely devastated." She faced Ben again. "If I had decided to stay in Calhoun Corners I was going to make the paper nonpartisan again. But there's no point to me staying—"

"I thought you wanted to keep the paper so your dad would have something to come home to?"

Jericho's voice came from behind her and Rayne nearly panicked. The Capriottis were formidable as individuals. As a group they were nearly overwhelming.

"I don't think my dad wants to come home."

"You don't know that," Elizabeth said, sliding her arm around Rayne's shoulders.

"Okay, what about this, then?" Rayne said, shifting away from Elizabeth. "Maybe I don't want to be around when he does come home."

Ben snorted a laugh. "I can understand that."

"Ben!" Elizabeth turned to Rayne again. "You're upset and I can see that you feel terrible about the election. But you were only doing your job."

Rayne laughed slightly. "You're not making my dad

look any better. Besides, even Jericho realized my dad set things up for me to move on. It's time I accepted that and did it."

"But your dad is your only family," Jericho said from his position at the door.

"Yeah," Rayne agreed, facing him. "And he used me. Worse, I should have been smarter. He made a damned fool out of me and for the past three weeks everybody's known it but me."

Ben said, "Now, come on, Rayne. That's not true," at the same time that Elizabeth said something equally sympathetic, but Rayne hardly heard them. Coming face-to-face with the truth that her dad had used her was bad enough. Realizing he'd made a fool of her was harder. But the worst was the way he'd made it so she wouldn't stand a chance with someone like Jericho Capriotti because he had always taunted his dad.

It really was time to move on, but this wasn't something she needed to discuss with the Capriottis. She was too filled with emotion. If she stayed she'd cry. And she'd already embarrassed herself enough in front of these people.

She pivoted away from Elizabeth and Ben and bolted past Jericho before he could stop her.

Rayne was pulling her car into the driveway of her house before Jericho caught up to her. He jumped out of his pickup and skipped two of the three steps of her porch so he could grab her arm, forcing her to an abrupt halt.

"This is wrong!"

"What? That my dad used me or that I was too damned stupid to see it?"

"That you're leaving!" He captured her shoulders and heaved in a breath to prevent himself from shaking her silly. "Damn it, Rayne! You can't take the blame for what your dad did! And if you leave now that's exactly what you'll be doing."

He stopped because Rayne was staring up at him with her pretty blue eyes. He didn't see the upset he had seen when she looked at him from across his father's den. He didn't see the tears that he knew had threatened in the final seconds before she shot out the door. He saw only awareness of their nearness and he didn't stop to think. He tightened his hold on her shoulders and yanked her to him so he could kiss her.

But after only a few seconds, she pulled back and gazed at him. Her eyes were filled with hope, so much hope that Jericho nearly cursed because, like an insensitive idiot, he'd given her the wrong idea.

But she must have read that in his expression, because she stepped away from him and without a second's hesitation, turned and unlocked her door. She slipped inside her house without offering him the chance to come in, letting him know she understood.

He might like her, but he didn't want to.

"Everybody's making too big of a deal out of this."

Jericho peered up from the stack of papers he was reviewing to see his father standing in his office doorway. "Too big of a deal out of what?"

Ben closed the office door before he said, "This election thing."

Realizing his dad's visit was personal, not an official Calhoun Corners matter, Jericho tossed his pencil to his desk blotter and leaned back in his chair. "I'm not sure I follow."

Taking the seat across from Jericho, Ben said, "I know that Mark Fegan tearing me apart in the papers seemed all wrong. But the truth is that's politics."

"You had just had a heart attack—"

"That's exactly my point! I had had a heart attack. The editor of the paper had the right to question my competency."

"But he only did it to get himself out of trouble."

Ben sighed. "Doesn't matter. I had had a heart attack and the townspeople had a right to wonder if I could still do the job."

Jericho chuckled. "Being mayor of a little town like this one isn't much of a job."

"It's still a responsibility," Ben said, shaking his finger at his son. "And the people of this town deserved a good mayor."

"And they've got one."

Ben took a long breath. "Jericho, you're missing my point. Everybody's angry with Rayne Fegan for what her dad did."

"She helped."

"She investigated, which is her job. It was the paper's job to hold me accountable. It was her job to follow her boss's orders."

"Okay," Jericho agreed, though he had no idea what his dad wanted.

"You heard her last night. She wants to leave. If people don't come back around to supporting the newspaper soon, she will leave. We'll not only lose our local paper, it will also look like I more or less ran the Fegans out of town."

Finally seeing that his dad was worried about being accused of something he didn't do, Jericho nodded. "I get it."

Ben rose with a sigh and began to pace Jericho's small office. "I don't think you do. I'm concerned with the fact that we could lose our newspaper."

"It's not much more than gossip."

"It's still our connection to each other. Having birth and wedding announcements, a place to put high school football scores and Mary Talerigo's recipes binds us. Makes us a unit." Ben faced Jericho. "We need that paper and I don't want her to go."

Jericho took a breath. "And what exactly do you want me to do about it?"

"I'm going to go around town this week and chat with the local business people."

Jericho nodded. "Sounds reasonable."

"As mayor I can't encourage them to take ads, but I can point out the town's loss if she goes and let them draw their own conclusions."

"Makes perfect sense." But still didn't explain what his dad wanted him to do. "What else?"

"If she comes to you for advice, I want you to encourage her to stay."

That would be the worst thing he could do. He'd already given her the wrong idea twice. Three times would be grossly unfair. "Dad, I can't."

"Yes, you can. And not because you're the only person in town she responds to, but because you started befriending her weeks ago. Before anybody realized how serious her problems were. You're the only person who can make it look like you really like her."

Running his hand down his face, Jericho said, "No."

"I'm not asking you as mayor. I'm asking you as your dad. Or maybe just another human being. She's all alone, Jericho. She needs somebody."

"That's the problem. She does need somebody. Somebody who really cares about her."

Ben shook his head. "And you think you don't? I was there last night when you ran after her when she left our house. I'm not sure why you came back so soon but if you're stopping yourself from being her friend because you think I want you to stay away, I don't."

When Jericho said nothing, Ben sighed. "I did not mean to hurt her last night. Had I realized how serious this problem was for her, I never would have been cool with her when she came to me. I can apologize for being insensitive last night and tell her I'll do anything I can to support her, but she needs a friend. You could be her friend."

When Jericho arrived at the paper offices that night, Rayne silently opened the back door and walked away. Behind her, she heard the soft click when the door closed and enough rustling that she knew he followed her to her front office. She took her seat behind her desk and said nothing as he sat on the chair behind the desk across from hers.

"We need to talk."

Rayne still said nothing as he slid the rim of his Stetson between his thumbs and forefingers, obviously nervous. She had no idea why he was here, but her heart pounded in anticipation. Nobody had ever been uncontrollably, irresistibly attracted to her the way Jericho seemed to be. When he'd kissed her the night before, she knew it had been because he couldn't stop himself. She should have been angry that he just ran away the way he did, but something inside her thrilled to the way he lost control with her. It was simple. It was elemental. It spoke of whispered words in the dark or long afternoons with nothing to do but make love.

Still, she wasn't an idiot. Their situation wasn't ideal. She was on the wrong side of an entire town and would probably have to close the paper and get a job in the city. If that wasn't enough, feuding fathers stood in the way of them doing anything about their attraction.

She didn't know if Jericho had come to remind her of those things, or to tell her he wanted to try to work out their situation, but either way, she felt as if her future was on the line.

Finally he said, "My dad came to see me this morning."

"Really?" She couldn't stop the pounding of her heart or control the trembling of her body, but she did manage to make her voice sound solid and strong. If he was here to tell her he couldn't have anything to do with her because he didn't want to be involved in her troubles, she wasn't going to look like a wimp or the sad little girl nobody wanted. *He* wanted her and if he was too stubborn to do something about it, she wasn't going to make rejecting her easy on him.

"Did he want to make sure you never talked to me, too?"

"Actually, he wants to make sure that I don't stop talking to you because of him."

Everything inside Rayne stilled. If his dad had no problem with their relationship, then that was one stumbling block gone.

"Not only does he think the entire election thing got blown out of proportion, but he thinks Calhoun Corners needs your newspaper and he doesn't want you to go."

The paper. Jericho hadn't come to her tonight to talk about them. He'd come to talk about the paper. Rayne struggled to control the sense of disappointment that squeezed her lungs. She refused to be needy.

"Too late. I sent out résumés today. As soon as somebody hires me, the paper closes."

"That's not right."

"Really? Though my father went about his attacks on your dad in a way that was a tad more personal than professional, as editor of the newspaper he had every reason in the world to question the competency of a man who had just had a heart attack. Yet, the whole town is behaving as if we committed a crime. We didn't. We did our jobs."

"That's what my dad said this morning."

"I never should have apologized to him last night. I was upset about my dad, the paper, and being dead broke and probably hated by at least fifty percent of the people in my own damned hometown. It was a mistake to let your dad think we thought we were wrong or that I was weak or that he could manipulate me simply by refusing to accept my apology."

"He figured out you had hit your breaking point last night. That's why he came to me. After the way I chased you, he knows I care about you."

Her chin lifted. "But not enough to have a relationship. To actually be seen with me in public."

"That's the difficult part of this situation. Your troubles with people in town and our feuding dads were a convenient excuse for me to keep stepping back, so I never had to be completely honest with you about why I didn't want a relationship."

"I'm sure you've got a great reason."

"My last girlfriend ran off with my best friend."

Though she felt a twinge of his pain, she pretended indifference. "How clichéd."

"Then you'll really love the fact that when they left I went on a drinking, gambling, fighting spree."

She shrugged. "At least you're predictable."

"And for once I like it."

That stopped her cold and she caught his gaze. "You liked drinking, fighting and gambling?"

"No. I like being predictable."

He smiled crookedly and Rayne's heart melted. He was without a doubt the most handsome man she'd ever met, but now that she was getting to know him she realized she liked his personality a lot better than his looks. He was strong enough to deprive himself of things he wanted to assure he had the things he believed in. He was smart enough to know the difference. All her life he had been one inch out of reach, and it appeared that the pattern continued.

"I like being safe. Normal. Trustworthy."

Continuing to feign indifference, she busied herself with stacking papers on her desk. "And being seen with me would make you unpredictable?"

"Being your friend would be fine." He caught her gaze. "Becoming lovers wouldn't."

Her whole body trembled when he said the word "lovers." Her pulse scrambled. Her limbs turned to mush.

"I had my experience with settling down with a

woman. I had to seduce her into my life and constantly jump through hoops to keep her happy."

"Sounds like a barrel of laughs."

"That's the point. It wasn't. I'm not a good person to live with. She was always upset with me because no matter how hard I worked at being a good partner I failed because it doesn't come naturally to me. I'm selfish. I'm stubborn. I don't remember birthdays. I don't bring flowers. I leave socks and towels on the floor."

Rayne laughed in spite of herself.

"You're way too nice for me to hurt you, Rayne."

This time tears filled her eyes, but she quickly blinked them back. "You're the only person in town who thinks I'm nice and the only damned person in town I wished didn't."

"Too late."

He smiled again and Rayne's chest contracted with pain. She didn't know why she responded to him. She had no clue why he responded to her. But their chemistry was killing her and she knew what she had to do.

"Yeah, well, I'm leaving town anyway."

"I wish you wouldn't."

She shook her head. "Your dad wishes I wouldn't. *You're* going to be glad to see me go."

He swallowed and rose from the seat across from her. "Not really. I think we could have been good friends."

"Yeah, I'm sure that our future spouses would love that."

"You don't have to worry about seeing me with a future spouse. I told you. I'm not marriage material."

She smiled sadly. "Right. One of these days a pretty

little girl who doesn't come with a boatload of trouble is going to sweep you off your feet and you'll forget all about the fact that you once liked me."

He shook his head. "I doubt it."

They stared into each other's eyes, as silence reigned, broken only by the tick of the old clock in her dad's office. His voice was so soft and sincere she had no doubt he genuinely regretted that they couldn't have a relationship.

"I've gotta go."

She shrugged. "Yeah, go."

"Let me know if you have any luck with your job search."

"Nah. No point."

"So one day the paper's just going to stop coming?"

She almost said, "What difference does it make?" Instead she said, "I'll print a farewell edition."

"I still think it's wrong for you to leave town. What about your plan to keep the paper open so that your dad has something to come back to?"

Rayne didn't reply. She pretended to be focused on proofing the hard copy of an article she had written about a church bake sale and eventually he turned and walked out of her office, through the back room, out the door and out of her life.

And Rayne dropped the paper she had been pretending to read. She let her eyes fill with tears. Her dad didn't want to come back. He hadn't even called to let her know he was okay. Not even on Thanksgiving. Christmas was fast approaching and she had nowhere to go. No friend who would refuse to let her spend the holiday in an empty house. No aunt, uncle or cousin who wanted her company. No Dad. No Mom.

It was time to get a life and she wasn't going to find one in Calhoun Corners. She had to leave.

Chapter Seven

Jobs were not as easy to come by as they had been when Rayne had first graduated from college. Every newspaper to which she applied had entry-level positions, but no mid-level. Luckily, even the most stubborn Calhoun Corners business owners began buying ads again, and everybody in town bought space in the paper to wish subscribers Merry Christmas. She was so busy that out of habit she fell back into wearing jeans and sweatshirts, and nobody seemed to notice or care. By the time January first rolled around, Rayne's bills were paid. She had food on her table. And her life seemed to have settled into a sort of routine.

Stomping the snow off her boots as she entered the diner the second Monday in January, she noticed Jericho sitting at a booth in the back and she waved to him.

"Good morning, Chief," she said, just as if she were any other Calhoun Corners resident because that was another thing that had settled in. She and Jericho had gotten comfortable saying hello. She hadn't tried her luck on an entire conversation, but if she was forced to stay in Calhoun Corners for any length of time, she couldn't avoid him forever. She also recognized that talking to him wasn't going to be easy.

She hadn't been kidding when she'd told him that some sweet young woman would sweep him off his feet. He was a handsome man with integrity. What woman wouldn't want him? And when the day came that somebody did catch his eye, Rayne had to be able to more than handle it. She had to be able to pretend she'd never had feelings for him and she was thrilled he'd found somebody. Or she'd forever be known as the spinster newspaper owner in love with the chief of police who didn't love her.

"Morning, Rayne," Elaine said as Rayne walked to the counter. "I have got the best idea for you."

"Really? Because all I came in for was coffee."

Elaine laughed. "You're such a kidder. You got the sense of humor everybody wished your dad would have had."

Accustomed to people making comments about her missing father, sometimes even derogatory comments, Rayne didn't react.

Elaine handed her a takeout container of coffee. "When I was at my sister's in Phoenix over the holidays, we went to a little diner for breakfast and they had place mats with advertising on them."

"Lots of restaurants do that, but there's no market for it here." Remembering Bert's reason for not even wanting to advertise in the newspaper anymore, she added, "This is a small town and everybody knows where the diner and hardware store are. There's no need to advertise what customers can see just by looking out the diner window."

"True, but if you went over a town, you could probably persuade those businesses to advertise here and I could get free place mats."

"You want me to sell advertising to businesses the next town over, so you can get free place mats?"

"And you could earn about five hundred dollars a month, if you did a new place mat every month."

"How do you think Bert's going to like that?"

"Bert advertises on a place mat in Olympia."

Rayne looked at her. "Are you kidding?"

Jericho came to the counter to pay. Handing his receipt and a five dollar bill to Elaine, he said, "I've seen it, too. When I was driving to Richmond on Route 64 once, I stopped for coffee and saw that Bert had his phone number in an ad on a place mat in a diner just off the interstate. I figured he had it there in case somebody broke down and was looking for a part he might have."

He turned and smiled at her, and Rayne's heart skipped a beat. She knew he didn't want the paper to close for the town's sake. His information was nothing but objective and impersonal, but any time he looked at her she melted.

"That makes sense."

"And it also makes sense for you to branch out." Jericho took his change from Elaine and pocketed the coins. "This might be the way to bring back your advertising salesman and potentially expand the number of ads you get in the paper."

"Wow, Jericho," Elaine said. "You're really good at this."

"Just trying to keep our paper in town," Jericho said, then slid his Stetson on his head. He caught Rayne's gaze again. "Every week it looks better, Rayne."

With that he walked out of the diner and Rayne stared after him. Forgetting about Elaine standing behind the counter, she watched him walk across the street and to the borough building.

"Remember when I told you that I thought you liking him was reaching for the stars?"

Rayne laughed, then faced Elaine. "Yes."

"Well, I changed my mind. Now that things have calmed down for his dad and Jericho himself has settled in, I think your hooking up is just a matter of timing."

"Not a chance."

"Maybe if you'd get rid of the glasses again and break out some of those pretty sweaters you were wearing around Thanksgiving, things would be different?"

Not about to tell Elaine she had tried that and failed, Rayne chuckled. "Right."

"Oh, come on, Rayne. Humor an old woman. At least give it a try."

"To amuse you?"

"Calhoun Corners is a dull town at best. In the winter, we're downright boring. Put your contacts in and get out that raspberry colored sweater and see what happens."

"You're nuts."

"It would probably help you sell advertising in the nearby towns if you went there looking like somebody with pizzazz."

"I have plenty of pizzazz."

"Not in that sweatshirt." Elaine smiled crookedly. "Please?"

Suddenly recognizing that Elaine might not be making the suggestion for Rayne to dress better to snag Jericho as much as to sell advertising so Elaine would get free place mats, Rayne sighed. "We'll see."

But the next morning she dressed in her raspberry sweater and white wool pants because she knew Elaine was right. A better dressed saleswoman would sell more ads and Rayne needed to sell as many ads as she could. If she wanted to save money to hire someone to search for her dad, she needed another source of income. Selling advertising for place mats for Elaine's diner was the perfect way to get cash quickly. To be successful at selling advertising for the place mats, she had to appear businesslike, yet still bright and cheerful. She wouldn't look any of those in worn jeans and a sweatshirt.

Elaine's eyes widened when Rayne walked into the diner, but she said nothing about Rayne's curly hair, contacts or pretty sweater. Rayne waved to Jericho. He waved back.

When she reached the counter, Elaine leaned close and said, "You look great!"

"I have out-of-town appointments." She took a breath. "I'm going to take your suggestion and sell advertising for place mats for you."

Elaine clapped her hands together with glee. "Oh, that's wonderful."

"Yeah, well, let's hope I'm not wasting a tank of gas."

"You won't be," Elaine promised. "Businesses like place mat ads because they're cheap."

"Do you happen to know how much they charge?"

Ringing up the sale for Rayne's coffee, Elaine said, "I think it's about fifty dollars an ad, with the people taking the corner ads paying a hundred. You can put about twenty ads on a place mat that way."

Rayne's eyes widened. "That could be a thousand dollars!"

Elaine nodded. "Your only real expense will be the printing and your tank of gas. The rest will be profit."

Rayne handed her coffee money to Elaine. "Wow. Wish me luck."

Elaine said, "Good luck."

From behind her, Jericho also said, "Good luck."

Happy, finally feeling as if she might be able to make enough money to begin saving for the search for her dad, Rayne spun to face him. "Thanks."

His gaze stalled on her face. "You're welcome."

He paid Elaine then quickly left the diner and Elaine laughed. "I'm telling you. That sweater is a killer."

Rayne shook her head as she picked up the coffee Elaine had set on the counter for her. "Right now all I'm interested in is making enough money that I can bring back a salesperson."

She walked out of the diner and was surprised when she stepped onto the sidewalk and Jericho was waiting for her.

"I really meant it when I said good luck in there."

She smiled. "I know."

"That's good," he said, but he didn't make a move to leave. Instead he continued to stare at her as if he expected her to say something.

Not able to think of anything, she only stared back, taking advantage of the opportunity to soak in every detail of his features. But when her gaze stopped on his eyes, she noticed that he was doing the same thing to her. It seemed ridiculous that they could have such strong chemistry, when they barely knew each other, but she suddenly realized that they knew each other a lot more than they had even the month before when he decided it wasn't a good idea for them to have a relationship.

They saw each other every morning. They knew each other's lives. He didn't feel uncomfortable putting in his two cents when Elaine made the place mat suggestion, and he not only encouraged her in the new venture, he also encouraged her about the paper.

But he had also said he didn't want to have a relationship. And it didn't appear that he'd changed his mind. And she wasn't chasing him. She was tired of begging for affection and attention. Her own parents had provided her with enough rejection.

She took a breath. "I gotta go."

"Okay," he said, then smiled briefly. "Good luck…again."

"Thank you." She paused long enough to salute him with her coffee. "Again."

With that she walked away, not stopping at the newspaper office, but going directly to her car, which was parked in a space behind the building.

She opened the lid of her coffee before beginning the drive, refusing to let herself think about Jericho, except to concede that once he made a decision he didn't deviate. And he certainly wasn't a man willing to take a risk. Of course, he thought he'd already taken a risk with the woman he lived with and she'd hurt him. So, in a way, Rayne understood his hesitation. Still, she'd been hurt. Her former boyfriend had all but destroyed her when he dumped her, but she was willing to try again.

She sighed and would have rested her head on her steering wheel had she not been driving up the entrance ramp for the interstate. She wasn't supposed to be thinking about Jericho, yet here she was, thinking. And why? Because she was more than willing to try again. She was desperate to try again. She wanted somebody in her life. She was tired of being alone. But more than either of those, she'd never before seen in anyone's eyes what she saw in Jericho's every time he looked at her, and she longed for somebody to want her the way he did. She understood his reluctance to get involved again. She really did. But she hated it. *He* was the man she needed. Somebody who looked at her with pure, unadulterated yearning and who was strong, smart and sexy.

On the verge of being angry with herself for not getting beyond this, Rayne saw a little red sports car stopped along the road. The car was unique enough that she immediately recognized it as Tia Capriotti Wallace's car. As she passed the vehicle, she glanced inside and saw Tia sitting with her head back and her eyes closed.

Traffic was sparse, so Rayne jammed on her brakes, eased her car to the berm, then hurriedly yanked her gearshift into reverse, driving back to Tia's car. When she was in front of it, she shoved her gearshift into park and jumped out.

She tapped on Tia's window but Tia didn't move. From the tightness in Tia's face, Rayne could tell she was in pain, so she grabbed the handle and pulled open the door. Tia was breathing heavily, gripping the steering wheel for dear life.

"Tia! What's wrong?"

"Rayne!" she gasped in between panting breaths. "I'm in labor. I can't drive. I can't think. Everything's happening so fast."

"Do you have your cell phone?"

"Yes, but it's not working! I don't know if we're in an out-of-service area or if the battery's dead, but it's not working!"

"Okay," Rayne said, hearing the panic in Tia's voice and forcing herself to stay calm. She'd long ago given up the expense of her own cell phone, but she also knew that if she stayed logical and unruffled, she could get Tia to the hospital. It was located just one block after the first turn off the interstate, only about ten miles up the road. "You're going to have to get into my car."

Tia nodded. "Okay." But she didn't move.

"Are you anywhere near the end of a contraction?"

"Dear God, I hope so."

"Okay, let me know when you can walk."

Tia panted a few more breaths, then nodded. "I think maybe now."

"Let's go quickly," Rayne suggested casually, praying she sounded sane and stable enough that Tia would trust her.

A half hour later, when Tia had been taken away in a wheelchair and Drew Wallace and Ben and Elizabeth Capriotti had been called, Rayne collapsed on a plastic chair in the emergency room waiting room.

She sat with her head bent, just breathing for at least

five minutes because she absolutely felt she had earned it. The hospital wasn't a long distance away, but Tia's pains kept coming increasingly closer. For a few minutes Rayne feared she would be delivering a baby that morning. But by staying calm and focused, she'd gotten Tia to the hospital on time. And she most certainly didn't feel like going to a bunch of businesses begging them to buy ads for a place mat.

"You okay?"

Rayne glanced up. "Jericho?"

"My mom called." He took a seat on the chair beside Rayne's. "She told me you found Tia on the side of the road."

She kicked the toe of his boot. "Lucky day for me to be on the interstate, huh?"

"Absolutely," he said so seriously that Rayne looked over at him.

She took a breath. "It was scary," she admitted, understanding that she could be honest with him. "But I also know that babies are born every day. I just kept telling myself that if I focused I'd get her here."

"You did good."

"I do a lot of good."

"I know."

"So does this win me any brownie points in the romance contest?"

"It isn't a contest." He looked away with a sigh and when he turned his gaze on her again, his expression was intense, serious. "I'm just not the settling down kind."

She laughed. "Oh, you are. When the right woman comes along you will snap her up."

"I don't think so."

"I know so. When you find the one who doesn't have the fatal flaws I have, you'll fall like a ton of bricks and be married before two months are up."

She stopped because he was looking at her as if she were crazy.

"You think you have a flaw that keeps me from liking you?"

"Of course. You're so attracted to me you can't look at me without thinking of sex, yet you refuse to do more than exchange a platitude or two. So, yeah. I pretty much figure I have a fatal flaw."

"*I* have the fatal flaw," he said, pointing at his chest. "I don't want to be in the position where I'm always apologizing for being who I am."

Ben Capriotti rushed into the emergency room, emerging from the corridor Tia had been taken down. Rayne hadn't even seen Ben arrive, but that didn't surprise her since she'd been preoccupied with settling herself down enough that she could drive to her appointments.

"Jericho! There you are!"

Both Jericho and Rayne rose from their seats. Jericho said, "How's Tia?"

"She's already had the baby—a girl," he said, walking toward them. He caught Rayne's hands. "Rayne, I can't thank you enough."

"Hey, I just did what anybody would do. I could see she was in trouble and stopped."

"She told me you backed up on the Interstate," Jericho said, facing her.

"Are you gonna arrest me?"

"He'll answer to me, if he even tries," Ben said,

putting his arm around Rayne's shoulders. "Come see the baby you saved."

"I didn't save her," Rayne said, brushing off his praise. "Honestly, Ben, somebody would have stopped eventually." She took a pace back, out from under Ben's arm. "You guys go see the baby. I need to get to work."

Jericho gaped at her. "You can't leave without seeing the baby!"

"I'll visit Tia after she's home," Rayne said, backing toward the big glass emergency room doors. "Besides, I've got to move my car. Don't want to be blocking the ER entrance for too long." She heard the automatic doors behind her open and turned and ran to her car.

No one appreciated the good fortune of having a close family more than someone who wanted one, too. But that was exactly why Rayne wouldn't interrupt their moment. She wasn't a part of things. Jericho didn't want her to be a part of things. She didn't want to spoil it for him.

So she got into her car which, without Tia, suddenly seemed quiet and dull. She almost laughed. Missing the panic of a woman in the throes of labor was a new level of loneliness for her.

Chapter Eight

When Rayne reached the intersection that would take her either back to Calhoun Corners or ahead to Tucker she decided that, as always, life went on, so she had to, too. She arrived at her first appointment an hour late and Alvin Davis, bed-and-breakfast owner, did not greet her happily.

"You're late."

"I know and I'm sorry. You're never going to believe this," she said, knowing the truth was always the best course of action. "But I stumbled on my friend on the interstate and she was in labor. I had to drive her to the hospital. For a while there I actually worried I was going to have to deliver her baby. Luckily, we made it on time."

Alvin, a sixty-something man with thinning white hair and a face that was probably pleasant when he smiled, looked skeptical. His wife, Theresa, a round woman with bottle-red hair and sparkling blue eyes, laughed with glee. "That's so funny."

Rayne grimaced. "I'm not sure I'd call it funny." Though now that she thought about it, the expression on her face as she raced Tia to the hospital had probably been worth the price of admission. "But I was glad I had appointments this morning that put me in her path."

Theresa motioned for Rayne to follow her into her kitchen. "I'll bet your friend was, too. Come on, you look like you could use a sweet roll."

"And a nap," Rayne said, suddenly realizing that she was emotionally drained.

"Saving people isn't work for wimps," Alvin agreed, warming up a little. "Do you prefer coffee or tea?"

"Coffee's great," Rayne said, taking a seat at the kitchen table. The house had the welcoming feel that Rayne expected to find in a bed-and-breakfast, but the kitchen was cozy. Warm. Home. Something she'd never had with a dad who collected anything and everything pertaining to subjects that interested him and a boy-friend who worried about appearances. Her apartment in Baltimore had been black and turquoise. Beautiful to be sure, but also startling. Certainly not warm. Definitely not home.

"Your kitchen is wonderful."

Theresa batted a hand. "Oh, it's a mess. After breakfast it's always like this."

Rayne smiled, then inhaled the rich scent of the coffee Alvin placed in front of her. "Oh, now that's wonderful!"

Alvin hovered by a seat at the table. "We like it."

Rayne took a sip of her coffee. "It's heavenly."

"And here's your sweet roll," Theresa said, set the pastry on the table, then took a seat beside Rayne. "Now, what can we do for you?"

Rayne chewed her bite of sweet roll, swallowed and said, "I'm here because I'm selling advertising for place mats to be used at the Tea Cup, Bill and Elaine Johnson's diner in Calhoun Corners."

Alvin grunted. "Why would we want to put an ad on place mats in another town?"

"So that people visiting relatives in Calhoun Corners, who don't want to spend the night with those same relatives will know there's a bed-and-breakfast just ten or so miles up the road." Rayne took another bite of sweet roll, enjoyed it, then said, "But we can talk about that later. What I'd really like to know is if you sell these?"

Theresa laughed. "You'd come here every morning for a pastry?"

Rayne glanced around. "I'd come here every morning for the atmosphere." She drew in a long breath. "I never realized how tired I was."

Alvin slowly made his way to the table and pulled out a chair. "You're Mark Fegan's daughter, aren't you?"

The towns were close enough that gossip typically ping-ponged back and forth, so Rayne wasn't surprised he knew who she was and nodded.

Theresa patted her hand. "We heard about your dad leaving and the paper staff being cut."

"It's okay. I'm getting back on my feet."

"It's no wonder you're tired." Alvin lifted his coffee mug. "Rumor has it that you single-handedly saved that paper."

"I wouldn't go that far."

"Why not?" Theresa asked with a laugh. "If it's true, why not?"

Feeling very comfortable with the older couple,

Rayne shrugged. "It just seems like I'm making my dad seem incompetent or something."

Theresa tilted her head. "You miss him."

"Of course, I miss him."

"Our two boys live out of state," Theresa said. "We've got grandkids in California and Kansas."

"So, you understand?"

"People don't always stay where you want," Alvin said with a grunt. "And you can't hold 'em back because you want them around."

"No, I guess you can't."

"The important thing," Theresa said, "is to hang on to the ones you have."

Rayne chuckled ruefully. "I have no brothers and sisters and my dad wasn't the most social man in the world so he was something of a loner in town."

"So you probably also don't have many friends," Theresa speculated.

"I'm making headway. I run the paper differently. I have coffee at the diner every morning. Say hello, that kind of stuff. But these things take time."

"Having an extra cash stream is a smart business move," Alvin said. "Something your dad never thought of." He caught her gaze. "You're moving on."

"I guess."

"And there's nothing wrong with that."

Rayne laughed. "I guess."

"So why don't you go home today and sleep. Then come back to Tucker tomorrow and sell your ads. Stop here first," Theresa teased, "and I'll give you a sweet roll."

Rayne rose from her seat. "You know what? I think you're right. I am tired."

"If it takes you two days to hit all the businesses," Alvin said, walking her to the door. "You can stop for a sweet roll both days."

When Rayne arrived home, there was a message from Jericho on her answering machine, as well as a message from the flower shop that Drew Wallace had sent her an arrangement that they could deliver to her house or her office. She decided to have the flowers delivered to her house and smiled when she read the thank-you note. Drew had gone from being an absolute loner to being so smitten with Tia that his life revolved around her. Apparently, now that Rayne had taken her to the hospital, she was in very good standing with Drew.

After canceling all of her ad appointments for the day, she did as Alvin and Theresa Davis suggested and went to bed. Feeling refreshed after a three-hour nap, she considered going to the office, but instead filled trash bag after trash bag with her father's saved articles and magazines. She boxed the books, then called the library telling them she was about to make a significant contribution. At nine that night she went to bed again and when she awakened the next morning it was with a sense of happiness she hadn't felt in two years.

She dressed quickly and didn't stop at the diner. Instead, she drove directly to Alvin and Theresa's, where French toast with warm apricot syrup awaited her. They bought a place mat ad, which she gave them for half price, and she promised to come back Saturday night for supper.

That night she finished cleaning her house with the unexplainable sense that she was closing out one phase of her life and entering another.

* * *

When Jericho saw all the lights burning in her house, he took a long breath then rested his head on his steering wheel. Damn fool woman. Her life was a mess. She'd looked to be on the verge of a breakdown the last time he'd seen her. She hadn't gone into the office since she'd driven Tia to the hospital. Hadn't even bought coffee at the diner. Was it any wonder that when a full day went by with no sign of her he'd been about crazy?

He slammed his gearshift into park and bounded to her front door where he didn't bother with her dignified doorbell, but pounded on the wooden frame.

When she answered, dressed in flannel pajamas, with her damp hair tumbling down her back, apparently just out of the shower, he didn't waste time on preliminaries and simply said, "Where the hell have you been?"

She laughed gaily. "Selling ads in Tucker! You would not believe the interest I got."

She motioned for Jericho to enter and began to lead him to her living room—which was clean. No, not just clean. It was different. If there had been accent pieces in the room before this Jericho hadn't seen them for the clutter. Now, the room with the old floral furniture that should have been dull somehow looked bright and cheerful. Red glass ornaments sat on the fireplace mantel and end tables, and paintings of landscapes hung on two of the walls.

"In fact, while I was talking with the town florist, the couple who owns Tucker's little corner restaurant found me and asked if I would do a similar place mat for them." She turned and grinned at Jericho. "I'm definitely going to have to bring back an ad salesman!"

Jericho said, "That's great."

Rayne gestured for him to sit on the sofa. "You don't really sound as if you think it's great."

He ran his hand along the back of his neck. "I've been worried about you for two days. It's a little hard to come down from that."

Obviously pleased by his admission, Rayne smiled. "You were worried? Really?"

"Our conversation at the hospital didn't end in the best place."

"Where did it end?"

He gaped at her. "You don't remember?"

"Jericho, I had just raced a woman who was in labor to the hospital. The whole drive I worried that I was going to end up delivering her baby. Things might have seemed in control by the time you arrived, but I was still a bit shell-shocked."

Not yet relaxed enough to sit, Jericho paced to the mantel, picked up a white ceramic angel and smiled at the small feather wings. "You cleaned up."

She nodded. "I was tired of living in a mess."

He faced her and cocked his head in confusion. "You lived here for nearly a year with your dad without being bothered by it."

She shrugged. "Yeah, but I was upset about my breakup." She paused and shook her head. "No, I wasn't upset. I was devastated. Distraught. And furious. I could have lived in a barn for the first few months I was home and not noticed."

He would think that was a convenient excuse for her behavior when she first arrived home, except the house was so different. A quick glance into the dining room didn't just show that it was clean, it also made him believe an entirely different person lived here. The once cluttered table was cleared and a white lace cloth covered the cherrywood table. The heavy drapes he remembered from his last visit had been removed. Clean white blinds replaced them. Everything about the house was now open, airy, clean, as if the person living here was making a fresh start.

He turned and smiled at her. "It's so different."

She motioned around the room. "This is me. I'm not a collector like my dad. I don't save every article that tickles my fancy. I like pretty things, like these angels," she said, picking up a pale blue one that sat beside the metal base lamp. "I prefer contacts to my glasses," she said, causing Jericho to realize how pretty she looked. "I eat Danish for breakfast, but watch everything else I eat for the rest of the day. And living in Calhoun Corners, there's no reason to work over ten hours in any given day. If something misses this week's edition of the paper it can go in next week. Everybody hears everything through the grapevine before I print it anyway."

Jericho laughed.

"So," she said, spreading her hands. "I'm fine."

"Yeah, you are."

"I was about to have some cocoa. Would you like some?"

He took a breath. He had just gotten off duty, but his parents didn't expect him to keep hours that would bring him home at a set time. He could spend a minute unwinding.

He shrugged. "Sure."

He followed her into the kitchen, which also sparkled

from a recent cleaning. Oak cabinets dominated the room. Red floor tile gave it color. "Now, I know how you spent the past two days."

"Two nights," Rayne corrected with a laugh.

"That's right. You spent the day selling ads."

"I spent most of the first day sleeping." Pulling a half gallon of milk from the refrigerator, she grimaced. "I can't really take credit for being so successful in Tucker. The day I took Tia to the hospital, I arrived at my first appointment shell-shocked. The couple I was meeting runs a bed and breakfast. Somehow I ended up eating a sweet roll in their kitchen and they convinced me to go home and get some sleep."

Jericho chuckled as she poured the milk into a pot and turned on a burner of the stainless steel electric stove. "That's an interesting way to get rid of a salesman you don't want to buy from."

She shook her head. "No. They weren't getting rid of me. The truth is they're two softhearted people who saw right through my big deal saleswoman act. They told me I needed food and sleep and to go home and get both and come back the next day."

"Did you go back?"

After retrieving mugs from a cabinet, she turned and smiled. "Yes. They gave me apricot French toast, bought a place mat ad and invited me to dinner Saturday night. And I also think they spread the word that I needed help, paving the way for all my sales."

"That's the nice thing about living in a small town. People take care of each other."

She nodded and set the mugs on a counter. "I think I forgot that living in Baltimore as long as I did."

He slid onto a stool beside the butcher block in the center of the room. "It took me about two weeks to remember," he admitted with another chuckle. "At first I got annoyed at everyone's interference. Then one day Mrs. Gregory's cat was lost and half the town showed up for a search party."

Rayne laughed with glee. "A search party for a cat."

"She's Mrs. Gregory's baby girl," Jericho said, knowing it was true because the old schoolteacher didn't have children. "When we found Cecilia," he said, referring to the cat, "and everybody was as relieved as if we'd found a lost child, it all came back like an avalanche. These are people who care for each other. They gossip. They nitpick. They want to know what everybody else is doing. But when the chips are down, they are here for each other."

Shoveling heaping spoons of cocoa into the mugs, Rayne smiled. "Yeah."

Without looking at him, she turned and snapped off the burner, grabbed a red-and-white-checkered pot holder and lifted the pot of warm milk. She looked soft, homey and very, very feminine, and for the first time in a long, long time Jericho relaxed.

"Thanks for this," he said quietly.

"What? A cup of cocoa?"

"No, five minutes to talk like a real person."

Obviously understanding, she nodded. "Even in a small town being chief of police isn't a low-stress job."

"Believe it or not I spend most of my time warding off people trying to pry information from me."

She peeked over at him. "Me, too." Handing him his mug of cocoa she said, "Want to go back to the living room?"

"Yeah. Sure."

He settled on the sofa again and watched Rayne as she looked at the chair. It took him a second before he realized there was no end table by the chair and with his cocoa on a coaster on the coffee table in front of him, he patted the cushion beside him. "Sit. I won't bite."

She grimaced. "Sorry. My dad wasn't much on furniture."

Not wanting to get into a discussion about her dad when he was feeling comfortable for the first time in what seemed like forever, he changed the subject. "So, I guess your ex was a real pain in the butt."

"Funny thing," Rayne said, setting her cocoa on a coaster as she sat on the opposite edge of the sofa. "Now that a little time has passed, I'm beginning to think he was normal."

"Oh, yeah?"

"We were really good for each other the four years in college and even our first year after, but now that I look back on things I can see he was struggling our entire last year together."

"Struggling?"

She turned on the sofa, putting her arm across its back and one knee on the cushion in front of her, getting comfortable. "When we first met, we shared a dorm room and expenses, and we also shared the goal of wanting to graduate. But when we graduated, he went to work for a corporation. I took a job at a newspaper. We worked different hours, had totally different goals. The only time our lives intersected was when he needed me to research a few things for him."

"That's why you thought he used you?"

She nodded. "I came to terms with the fact that any one of my friends could have asked the same kind of favor and I wouldn't have thought it unreasonable, then inch by inch I realized that Nick and I had simply grown apart. Cleaning today, I even had some plesant memories." She smiled. "It's odd, but it feels good to know I can file him away."

"Well, you're about seven steps ahead of me. I don't think I'll ever file away Laura Beth."

She tilted her head in question. "You still love her?"

"No. God, no! But remembering her keeps me from making the same mistake twice."

"It probably also keeps you from trusting anyone."

He frowned, wondering how they'd suddenly tumbled into a conversation about him, but also realizing it didn't feel odd or even awkward to talk about Laura Beth with her.

"The woman I thought I would marry ran off with my best friend. If nothing else, that reminds me that I'm not a good judge of character."

"And you don't want to have to change," she said, raising her eyes heavenward, as if she thought his reasoning ridiculous.

He chuckled, glad that she felt comfortable teasing him. "No, I don't want to have to apologize for being who I am," he corrected. "I also don't want to hurt somebody just by being myself. Especially not you," he admitted, glad they were getting this out in the open because he wanted to be friends with her. He needed this kind of openness with someone and nobody else in this town had really had the kinds of experiences he and Rayne had had. It was odd, but they were very similar.

They'd both left town, gotten educated, become successful and lost the person they considered the love of their life. Instinctively he knew nobody could understand him or his life the way Rayne could. "You've been hurt enough."

"And you don't want to get hurt, either."

He couldn't deny it. "No. Who does?"

"You're not even willing to take the risk that I might be the kind of person who could tolerate living with you and wouldn't end up hurting you?"

He'd never thought about taking the risk that she might like him exactly the way he was and wouldn't hurt him. Just letting the idea pass through his brain gave him an odd syrupy feeling. His long-held fantasy melted with the real woman he was coming to know and like, and crazy feelings erupted inside him. Arousal. Warmth. Happiness. Genuine happiness.

He leaned forward and kissed her.

He expected the kiss to feel wrong or at least dangerous, as it had the other two times he'd kissed her. Instead it felt wonderfully right, and he couldn't understand why he'd been so hesitant to get involved with her. Everything inside him seemed to respond to her. He had a sense that he could never tire of her, never tire of looking at her or sleeping with her, if only because the better he knew her, the more he wanted her. If the ringing in his ears was anything to go by, she could just about knock him for a loop with a simple kiss.

It took a second before he realized that the ringing noise was the phone. He pulled away. Gazing into her pretty blue eyes, knowing he could get lost in them and lost in her, he whispered, "Don't you want to get that?"

"No."

He laughed. "Get it. It could be someone important."

She slowly unraveled herself from the sofa and reached to the end table to pick up the portable phone. "Hello?"

Jericho sat quietly, trying to sort out his feelings, but when she gasped, "Dad?" everything inside him froze.

"Dad, where are you?" she asked, bouncing from the sofa.

Confusion, curiosity and anger warred inside Jericho. Everybody in town was curious, if only about where her father had gone. Most people wondered why he'd never even called his daughter.

It was his anger that didn't make any sense. Particularly since he couldn't stop it. Everybody in town was coming to accept that though Mark Fegan's motives were bad, critical editorials were part of an election. Having been out of town for the entire debacle, Jericho hadn't even seen what Mark had written. So he shouldn't be angry. But he was. He was furious. He hadn't ever liked Mark Fegan. To Jericho, Mark using his power against a man who was sick was actually an illustration of the greater problem. Fegan didn't have a heart or a conscience. Using and then deserting his own daughter was the real proof of that.

He didn't know if Mark Fegan's call had come at the absolute worst time or the absolute best time, but he did know that a relationship between him and Rayne was not as simple as two people liking each other, enjoying each other's company or even wanting to be together.

She loved her dad. She wanted him in her life. But Mark Fegan wasn't a nice man. If Jericho started a relationship with Rayne, her father would be at every Capriotti function from baptisms to funerals. Jericho's family would always be on edge, wondering if this was the time Mark would become belligerent and start a fight.

Jericho wouldn't turn Rayne against the only family she had. That wouldn't be fair. He also wouldn't put her in a position of having to endure the humiliation of her father becoming the family embarrassment.

Seeing that she was focused on the conversation, Jericho recognized there was always a chance her dad wasn't coming home. But he also knew that she had missed her dad and he shouldn't try to cut her conversation short and his very presence might do that. No point in him staying. He'd have to wait until he saw her the next morning to know if he should let himself feel what he wanted to feel for her, or if he should quietly step aside.

Chapter Nine

When Rayne saw Jericho at the diner the next morning, she nearly walked over and took a seat at his booth. But she couldn't. She knew she couldn't. He liked her best when she was happy, normal, uncomplicated, and this morning she wasn't any of those. So pretending to be in too much of a hurry to pause to chat, she smiled and waved from her position at the counter in front of the cash register, then turned away.

The night before they'd shared their first real kiss. Jericho hadn't kissed her to prove a point or even to demonstrate that his attraction for her was something odd and out of control that he wasn't sure he wanted. He'd kissed her because he liked her. And why did he like her? Because she'd been relaxed and comfortable in a home that was of her own making and her own taste. He'd seen her quiet, comfortable, confident. At her best. Or at the very least at her most normal. Not somebody so poor she couldn't eat, so empty and alone she was sarcastic and snippy. But her real self. Her strong self. The woman he liked. Then her father had called and her entire world had fallen apart.

Her "hello" was barely out of her mouth when her father had blurted that he was done. He'd taken responsibility for her mother's family's newspaper for decades and he'd run from the loan shark, rather than try to figure out a way to pay his debt because he just couldn't take it anymore. The good news was that his breakdown wasn't about Rayne. She was an adult with an education, who could go anywhere and do anything, so he had simply assumed she would move on when he did. He'd told her that she'd been an enormous help for the year she had been home, but when he couldn't pay the loan shark the burden of the failing newspaper had become too much to bear.

Rayne had hastened to tell him that she'd not only paid off his loan shark, but also she was making the business profitable again. Advertisers were coming out of the woodwork, not just to put ads in the paper, but also seeking a spot on one of several place mats she was creating each month.

But he'd told her he was done. Finished. He was tired of being the responsible one and he wanted to be free. He wanted to see what life was like when you were the one drawing the paycheck and somebody else had all the responsibility.

Understanding that, Rayne told him that the paper would be there for him when he returned, but he'd exploded and said he didn't want to return. Ever.

Rayne had to concede that she understood that, too.

Her dad had never been popular in Calhoun Corners and after his incessant questioning of Ben Capriotti in the weeks before the election, he was very close to being hated. She accepted everything he told her and wouldn't have been too upset, except he wouldn't tell her where he was. He assured her that he was fine. He didn't want her to worry. But he also didn't want her to find him. He didn't want *anybody* to find him. Then he'd hung up.

Throughout the restless night, Rayne had told herself she didn't blame her dad. He wasn't well liked. Calhoun Corners reminded him of his failures. And he did have a right to make a new life while he was still young enough to enjoy it.

Intellectually, she understood. Emotionally, she was spent. She was especially tired of being left behind, being dispensable. Keeping his whereabouts a secret was the same as saying she wasn't welcome in his life.

Jericho rose from his booth and came over to pay his bill as Elaine handed Rayne her cup of coffee. She smiled a silent greeting, hoping he wouldn't question her, and turned to leave the diner, but he caught her arm.

"Can we talk?"

In Baltimore, when Rayne was working her way up the ranks at the newspaper where she worked, when she had always dressed well and had tons of friends, she would have swept this man off his feet. In Calhoun Corners, she couldn't get her act together. She wouldn't sweep him off his feet because every time she thought she might have a shot, her life fell apart, and she couldn't stop being another problem to him.

"Rayne?"

"We can talk," she said, though she knew she wouldn't tell him anything. What would telling him accomplish, except to make her look like a needy fool? "Pay your check and you can walk me to the paper office."

He said, "Okay," gave his money to Elaine and put his hand on the small of Rayne's back as they walked to the exit.

The bell tinkled when he pushed open the door and directed her outside. She stepped onto the sidewalk, hardly noticing the frigid January air that burned the inside of her nose.

Jericho rubbed his hands together. "Sure is cold."

She nodded and headed toward her building. It really was her building now. In the course of their phone conversation, her dad had told her that he had been considering selling the building. He'd told her that he believed the paper was worthless, but the building had value—if nothing else, the lot did. However, since she was making a go of the paper he'd decided to deed everything to her. This way if the paper failed, she'd still have the monetary value of the building. All things considered, her dad hadn't really abandoned her. In fact, he'd given her his only two assets. His home and the building for the *Chronicle*. She shouldn't feel too empty and alone.

"Yeah. It's freezing."

They walked a block in silence. Finally, Jericho sighed. "I'm sorry for leaving without saying goodbye last night, but I knew you would probably want to talk to your dad for a while."

She shrugged. "Yeah, we talked for a long time."

Jericho kicked the snow. "Good."

She nodded. "Yeah. It was a good talk." And she really, really wanted somebody to discuss it with. She longed for someone she could fall apart with, someone who would listen and understand what it felt like to be left alone, but she refused to be in a position again where Jericho would pity her. She didn't want his pity. She wanted him to love her, respect her, honor her. Instead she was nothing but the village idiot. "I've gotta get going."

"Okay." He caught her gaze.

Knowing she had to push herself through this without anybody's help, she smiled broadly, as if she didn't have a problem in the world. Let Jericho think her dad had told her where he was. Better yet, let him think her dad was coming home.

"I've got lots to do today. You know," she said, gesturing with her hands, not really saying anything substantial, but enough that he'd draw his own conclusions, "with my dad and all."

"Yeah, there's probably lots to do at the paper."

"And at home. If nothing else, it might take me all day to figure out how I'll explain giving away his books and burning half his articles."

Jericho laughed. "I'll bet."

She nodded. "So I guess I'll see you around."

Holding her gaze, Jericho said nothing for a few seconds, then finally he smiled slightly and said, "Yeah."

Rayne could feel tears welling in her eyes. Why did her life have to be such a mess? Why couldn't she be in a position where she could flirt and tease and make this man beg for her attention?

She had no idea why fate was tormenting her, but it was. Still, she smiled brightly before she walked away.

At her building door, she took out her keys and unlocked it. Stepping inside the main room of what was now her business, Rayne looked around. This was it. This was what she had left of her life.

Glancing from desk to desk, she wondered if her dad was right. Was she only picking up a family burden?

She would have forgotten her Saturday night dinner invitation from the Davises except Alvin called. "Theresa wanted me to remind you about dinner."

Rayne winced. "Sorry, Alvin. But I've been busy."

"You still have to eat. Theresa's been cooking all day. I'm not taking no for an answer."

With that Alvin disconnected the call and Rayne placed her receiver in the phone's cradle. Because it was already three o'clock and she'd been working since seven that morning, she rose from her seat. As if on autopilot, she drove home, took a long bath to relax her back and dressed in jeans and a sweater. Alvin met her at the door before she knocked.

"Come in! Come in!"

She entered the foyer of the bed-and-breakfast, the scent of roast beef wafted to her and her stomach rumbled. She smiled her first real smile in days.

Obviously having heard her stomach, Alvin smiled, too. "See that. I told you you needed to eat!" He turned toward the kitchen and yelled, "Theresa! Rayne is here."

Rayne glanced around the foyer, looking at the family pictures scattered about. "Are these your kids?"

"Yep. These are pictures for the past ten years. It's a tradition now. Every year each son takes a picture of his respective group when on vacation and at Christmastime and we put the photos around the rooms." He smiled proudly. "The newer the picture, the closer it is to the front door. It's like a slice of their lives for us."

Rayne picked up a photo of a handsome man with a pretty red-haired wife and three kids with missing teeth.

Alvin winced. "Oh, that was a bad year for the twins. Eleven through thirteen are awkward years for girls."

"I very painfully remember that because I lived it."

Alvin laughed and led Rayne into the kitchen where Theresa was setting the roast on the table. "You don't mind eating early?"

"She needs to eat early," Alvin said. "I heard her stomach rumbling when I took her coat."

"Then my timing is perfect!" Theresa pointed to a seat and said, "You sit here, dear."

They spent the next few minutes passing hot rolls, mashed potatoes, glazed carrots and roast beef around the table. Alvin said a quiet grace and Theresa happily said, "Amen! Let's dig in."

Rayne laughed, fully relaxing.

"So what happened in the past few days that made you sound so tired on the phone?" Alvin asked, making conversation.

Rayne smiled and said, "Nothing much."

"Oh, dear, your shoulders are too tight," Theresa said solemnly. "Something had to have happened."

Shaking her head, Rayne said, "You're too observant."

"We see a lot of people in and out of here. We know the signs," Alvin said, then took a bite of roast beef.

"Yeah, I guess." Rayne drew a quick breath. There really was no sense hiding from the truth. "My dad called. He doesn't want to come home, even though I told him I paid his debt and found a way to make the paper profitable."

"So he's running?" Alvin said.

"I think it's more that he's tired of working to provide jobs for others, and wants to find out what it's like to work for somebody else and have real free time and an actual paycheck."

Theresa considered that, then said, "Makes sense to me."

"I makes sense to me, too." Rayne shrugged. "At least logically."

"But emotionally you're having doubts?" Theresa asked.

"It's not really doubts. I feel empty."

Alvin said, "You need a guy."

At his complete lack of guile, Rayne laughed. "Oh, really?"

"I think so, too," Theresa said. "You're what? Twenty-four? Twenty-five?"

"Twenty-four."

"And you're about to take over the business," Alvin said. "Probably make it your whole life."

"I don't want to do that," Rayne said. "It was my dad's whole life and look where he is."

"Which is exactly why you need a fella." Theresa reached for her coffee. "Life's all about balance, but without somebody to balance with, you won't find time for anything but work because work will always seem more important, more pressing." She took a sip of coffee, then asked, "Is there somebody?"

"No."

"Of course, there's somebody," Alvin scoffed. "Otherwise you would have taken the first road out of Calhoun Corners and never looked back."

"I stayed so my dad would know he still had the paper to come home to."

"So why aren't you going now that he's called and said he doesn't want to come home? Why didn't you pack Friday morning and head out of town?"

"My dad said he was turning over the business to me."

Theresa caught her gaze. "So why didn't you tell him not to?"

Rayne closed her eyes. Why hadn't she?

Alvin chuckled. "So who is he?"

"Jericho Capriotti."

"Oh, the new chief of police," Theresa crooned. "I hear he's cute."

"He's very cute," Rayne said with a laugh. "And out of my league."

"Nobody's ever out of your league, kid," Alvin said, pointing his fork at her.

Theresa said, "He's right, Rayne. If you like this guy and he likes you, you need to make a move."

Alvin shook his head. "That's not the way to go about it. No man wants a woman he thinks is too available. You've got to somehow make yourself irresistible while making him think you're off limits."

As if it were that simple. Rayne just barely kept herself from rolling her eyes heavenward. "Right."

"It's like this," Alvin said, gesturing with his fork. "You've got to ignore him for a time, then be somewhere like a party together."

"His brother's wedding is coming up. February 14."

"That's good. It will give you a chance to dress really pretty," Theresa said.

Rayne shook her head. "I left out something important in this story. The day after my dad called, Jericho walked me to work. He was fishing for information about the phone call but I didn't want to tell him my dad wasn't coming home." She wasn't exactly sorry that she hadn't poured out her troubles to Jericho. That was the only way to preserve at least a little of her dignity. But now that she had worked through the emotions of her dad not coming home, she realized what she had said that day and how she had behaved might have been a bit extreme.

"Ever since Jericho returned to Calhoun Corners my life has been a mess. I didn't want any more of Jericho's pity, so I didn't tell him about my dad and the way the conversation ended it looked like I was giving him the brush-off."

"Doesn't matter," Alvin said. "In fact it might actually make you more interesting that you sort of gave him the boot."

Rayne laughed at his typical optimism, but Alvin continued. "Now what you have to do is go to his brother's wedding dressed like a knockout, then flirt with everybody else at the wedding but him."

Rayne gaped at him. "Isn't that counterproductive?"

"Nope. Make him think you're the girl every man wants and he'll want you, too."

Rayne grimaced. She wished she had enough courage or confidence to flit around the wedding reception making Jericho jealous. "Sorry, but I can't do that."

"Of course you can," Theresa said at the same time

that Alvin said, "We've got almost a month of Saturday night dinners to talk you into it. You think you screwed things up, but you actually set the stage by looking disinterested. Now he needs a little push. But you don't push by flirting with him, you make him come to you and he will."

Rayne took a breath. She had to admit Alvin's idea sounded like something she might have done in Baltimore, back when she had confidence. And she was tired of being a loser. Maybe it was time to take a positive step? To do something productive.

"Besides," Alvin said, suddenly serious. "It's better to look ahead than backward. You can't forget your dad. But he's your past. This Jericho guy, he sounds like your future. Smart people forget the past and go after their future."

Rayne had no trouble ignoring Jericho for the next few weeks. Busy with the place mats, bringing back one of her salespeople and writing each week's edition of the paper, she didn't have time to seek him out. As Rick's best man, Jericho appeared to be equally occupied.

The Saturday afternoon of Rick and Ashley's Valentine's Day wedding, as Rayne stood in front of her closet, looking at her choices for wedding attire, she stumbled upon the red dress. The one she guessed Jericho must have seen her wearing at the party in Baltimore.

She pulled it out. She wasn't entirely sure why it was such a showstopper to men. It wasn't low cut. It also wasn't all that short. Only an inch or two above the knee. She slipped into it and studied herself in the mirror. The simple sheath flowed over her curves and, without being overt, accented her tiny waist. Stopping an inch or two above the knee it also hinted that she had good legs. Other than those two things, though, a guy was on his own. The dress was so simple men had to use their imaginations to find it sexy. Still, if Alvin was right, men liked that.

Satisfied with her choice of dress, she applied makeup, then removed the electric rollers she had put in her hair and carefully brushed the long locks so the curls would be loose and disorganized.

Though it was cold, the snow had melted and the sidewalks were clear, so Rayne put on her highest red heels, grabbed her red-sequined clutch bag and slid into her black wool coat.

She walked to the church and sat quietly in one of the back pews as the happy couple exchanged their vows. Wearing a strapless white gown with elaborate beading, Ashley was stunning. With his black hair and piercing blue eyes, Rick was his usual handsome self in his black tux. But Jericho looked amazing. He didn't have Rick's playboy good looks. Instead he had the intense, mature appearance of a man of purpose and power.

Right then and there Rayne realized her friends the Davises were correct. He was the man for her. Not because he was handsome, though he was. Not because he was sexy, though he was sexy in spades. But because he was mature. Serious. He was a man of purpose and power, and though her crush might have been what had initially drawn her to him, it was his integrity that kept her from being able to forget him.

In the quiet church, Rayne realized she might have

lost her illusions about changing the world, but today, she suddenly saw that maintaining the peaceful environment in a town where a family could raise children was a trust not to be ignored. In a sense, as the owner of the newspaper and the chief of police, she and Jericho had been called to assure this town stayed as it was for the next generation. They were partners of a sort. That was why they understood each other.

After congratulating the bride and groom on the church steps, Rayne skillfully sidestepped greeting Jericho who had turned to speak with another of the groomsmen. She didn't want him to see her in her simple black wool coat. She wanted him to see her when she walked into the country club ballroom, without a coat, surefooted on floor rather than potentially icy church steps. She wanted her hair to be perfect. Her makeup without flaw.

She wanted him to feel what she always felt when he walked into the room, and if it took a sort of entrance to accomplish that, then so be it.

At the country club she met Bert in the parking lot, Elaine and Ron in the coatroom, Mrs. Gregory in the reception line, and all of the giggling high school cheerleaders in the rest room and realized that she wasn't going to walk into the ballroom alone. The lights wouldn't dim on her arrival. No spotlight would hit her. The band wouldn't strike up a tune.

This was Calhoun Corners.

She sat at a table for eight with Elaine and Ron, Janie Alberter, owner of the dress shop, Pete Forwalt, her rehired salesperson, and his wife, Millie and a couple who introduced themselves as the Maitlands, friends of Gene Meljac from New York city. Millie mentioned that she loved Rayne's hair. Elaine told her red was a good color for her, but otherwise nobody fussed over her appearance.

They ate dinner chatting about the happy couple, the happy parents of both the bride and groom, and the general state of the economy, and while everybody was finishing dessert Rayne glanced down at her dress. It didn't have a low neck. It wasn't short. Or tight. Or really anything special and she shook her head.

She was insane. Not only had she dressed for a man who appeared quite capable of ignoring her, but also she had to wonder about the memory of the man in question since her dress hadn't as much as gotten one compliment. Yet it had driven him to fantasies.

The band began to play. Rick and Ashley danced the first dance. Ashley danced the second dance with her father. Then Ashley announced her dad's engagement from the bandstand and that the next dance was for him and his fiancée, a pretty thirty-something brunette. The band then played a slow tune and Elaine and Ron and Pete and Millie joined Ben and Elizabeth Capriotti on the dance floor.

Sighing, Rayne made her way to the bar. Because she was driving she could only have one drink and she decided she needed it now. She walked up to the white leather bar, told the tuxedo-clad bartender she wanted a whiskey sour and studied the array of liquor bottles that lined the back wall.

"I like your dress."

Since there was apparently only one person on the entire planet who liked her dress, Rayne knew it had to be Jericho beside her. Wanting to pop him for steering her wrong, she turned to tell him he was the only one who liked her dress, but when she saw him her breath caught.

Leaning against the white leather, with a crooked sexy smile and his brown hair casually brushing his forehead, he looked about as good as a man could look. And everything Rayne wanted to say flew out of her head. The only thing that came out of her mouth was, "This old thing."

"I have some very good memories involving that old thing."

Rayne sighed and took the drink the bartender handed her. "You're the only one. Look," she said, holding out her leg. "It falls almost to my knee." She yanked at the round neck. "I'm not showing cleavage." She pivoted. "And there's a full back. What the devil did you find attractive?"

"Maybe I'm just a guy who likes to unwrap the package."

Rayne's heart skittered to a stop. *He was flirting with her!* Alvin was right. Even if Jericho had thought she'd given him the brush-off the day after her father called, he still liked her. She hadn't ruined everything.

"Want to dance?"

"Yes," she whispered, but her feet didn't move.

Jericho chuckled, took her drink from her hand, set it on the bar and led her to the dance floor. He pulled her to him and as if in slow motion she felt every inch as their bodies came into contact. He nestled her closer, resting his chin against her temple and Rayne's breathing stuttered.

"I'm glad you came."

"Huh?"

He pulled away and smiled down at her. "I'm glad you came. You've been sort of a hermit for the past few weeks."

She stared at him, studying his eyes, finally comprehending that he really was paying attention to her. Not only that, but he liked her. She could see a sort of amused affection in the depths of his pretty green eyes.

Boy, she owed Alvin big time for his advice.

She swallowed. "I needed some time to get adjusted to everything my dad told me."

"Yeah. So I hear you're a business owner now?"

She liked the fact that he hadn't come right out and confronted her about her dad not coming home. Saying she was a business owner was a much more positive way to admit he'd heard the gossip and he understood. Plus, the truth of her new status sort of swirled through her as they waltzed around the circular dance floor of the country club. She wasn't an abandoned daughter. She was a business owner. And the business wasn't failing as it had been while her dad ran it. And she felt a sacred trust to the town. She wasn't downtrodden or burdened. She was okay. No, she was more than okay. She was a successful business owner.

She suddenly wondered if it wasn't her dad's lack of passion for the little paper and the town itself that had prevented him from seeing the opportunities, then decided she didn't care. Whatever her father had done or hadn't was the past. She was moving on. And she was doing it well.

She stood a little taller. "More important to you, I'm a citizen of your town. You better watch your step around me, buddy, because I won't hesitate to complain to the mayor."

Jericho laughed. "I think this dress makes you funny."

"No, I've always been funny." She had been. In Baltimore, making people laugh was her claim to fame. "You just came home when I was going through a life crisis. I like to laugh. I like to joke. And I don't like this dress. I think you're the only one who does."

He tightened his hold on her. "Good."

Rayne shifted back so she could look at him. "Have you been drinking?"

"No," he said, then he lowered his voice. "I just spent two weeks thinking about you. Missing you. Tonight I realized that if I don't do something about that soon, some other guy will."

Rayne glanced around looking for either a wicked stepmother, fairy godmother or a big clock about to strike midnight. Alvin's advice might have had merit, but all of this was absolutely too good to be true.

The music ended, and though they parted to applaud the band, Jericho immediately took her hand again when they stopped clapping. He led her off the floor and over to his parents, who were standing on the edge of the dance floor watching Rick's one-year-old daughter Ruthie.

"Good evening, Rayne," Elizabeth said, then hugged her. "Thank you for coming."

"Thank you for inviting me," Rayne said as Ben reached around his granddaughter and extended his hand to shake hers.

"I understand you're the town's newest member of the chamber of commerce."

Rayne nodded.

"Her dad gave her the business," Jericho supplied before Rayne could.

Ben murmured his approval, but Ruthie squirmed in his arms. "Hey, little girl. You be nice or Pap won't dance with you."

"Why don't you let me take her?" Jericho said, reaching for her. "Rayne and I will show her the cake."

At that point, Rayne surreptitiously pinched herself. The pain she felt confirmed that she wasn't dreaming. Ruthie wrapped herself around Jericho and he kissed her temple.

Rayne smiled. "You're very good with her."

"I adore her. Mom baby-sits her and Tia and Drew's little girl a lot, and they're spoiling me."

"Don't you mean you're spoiling them?"

"No," he said, catching her gaze over Ruthie's little head. "They're spoiling me. There's nothing like the unconditional love of a child and I'm beginning to realize that I wasted a lot of years not knowing what I was missing."

Held in his mesmerizing gaze, Rayne's entire body quivered. He wanted kids. He wanted to settle down. He was choosing her.

Chapter Ten

They remained together for most of the wedding, until best-man duties took Jericho away. Knowing he would be tied up for the rest of the evening with those things, Rayne stayed until the last song played by the band, then quietly drove home.

Making herself a cup of cocoa before she would go upstairs, change out of her dress and slide into bed, she thought she couldn't be any happier until she heard a knock at her door. She opened it and there stood Jericho. His tie loosened, leaning against her door frame.

"Want some company?"

Lord. He looked about as good as any man could look, but that wasn't what spiked Rayne's blood pressure. The hour was late, which meant this was the kind of special visit a man only paid to a woman he wanted to sleep with.

She swallowed. Though she knew she wouldn't turn

him away, she couldn't deny being nervous and afraid. She adored this man. He was coming to realize he liked her, too. If she turned him away out of fear, she could lose him. If she didn't do everything right, she could lose him.

If she were perfect, making love with him would solidify their relationship. Since she wasn't, it was a roll of the dice. A big risk. One she had no choice but to take.

She stepped away from the door. "I'd love some company."

He smiled and Rayne's throat tightened. She wanted him so much that the risk suddenly seemed absolutely worth it.

"I was making cocoa, if you'd like some."

He strolled to her counter, looking sexy, sophisticated and so right in her house. When he turned and smiled at her, Rayne could have sworn she felt her bones melt.

"I'm really not in the mood for cocoa."

He walked over to her, slid his hands on her waist and pulled her close. "I was thinking of something a little hotter." With that he touched his lips to hers.

Rayne knew that if he hadn't been supporting her, she would have collapsed. Still, she forced herself to sound stable and strong when she said, "Let me turn off the burner and we'll go into the living room."

One of Jericho's hands left her waist and Rayne heard a quick snap. He'd managed to find the knob for the stove and turn it without missing a beat in kissing her.

"Wow. You're very good."

He chuckled low in his throat. "You haven't seen anything yet."

Though Rayne wasn't sure how they did it, they

managed to get to the living room without once ever stopping kissing, though Jericho had removed his jacket and she'd kicked off her shoes.

They half sat, half fell on the sofa and Jericho's lips slid from her mouth, down her throat. "I never thought we stood a chance."

Fighting a shiver, Rayne couldn't argue that. "Neither did I."

"Who would have believed that something bad like your dad deciding never to come home could pave the way for something good, like us being together?"

It wasn't his question that took Rayne so much by surprise that she froze; it was the implication behind it. At first she told herself she could be reading too much into it and should ignore it, but something inside her wouldn't let her.

"You only want me because my dad isn't home?"

He spoke between soft, wonderful kisses that he pressed to her neck. "It's not quite that cut and dried."

Accept it. Accept what he's saying. Don't be upset over something you have no control over. Don't lose this!

"It sounds cut and dried to me."

"Don't be silly."

It was very hard to keep a train of thought when someone was nibbling her earlobe, but Rayne struggled to do just that. "Okay, if it's not completely cut and dried, then answer this. If my dad were here or if he'd called the other week to say he was coming home, would we be here right now?"

He stopped and peeked at her. "Here?"

"I don't mean here in this house. I mean, would you have danced with me tonight?"

"Yes." He paused, then said, "Maybe." He squeezed his eyes shut. "No. Probably not."

"Because you don't like my dad?"

Sighing, he leaned back on the sofa. "Rayne, even you know your dad is a problem."

She shook her head. "A problem is when you don't have enough money to pay the rent or the neighbor's cat leaves rodents under your back porch. My dad is my dad. My family."

"And he's not here right now, so it seems stupid to have this discussion."

"Not really," Rayne said. Despondence washed over her. She'd thought he liked her, but he didn't. Forced to really dissect what he had said at his brother's wedding reception about wanting to settle down, she suddenly saw that what he liked was the idea of getting married. His family now loved her because she'd driven Tia to the hospital when she was in labor. Plus, without her father she was a successful businesswoman, someone growing in popularity in the town in which he was chief of police. In a sense they'd be the perfect couple. She'd even thought the same thing herself in the church when she realized they held a sacred trust to the town.

She swallowed hard. "You don't like me."

Jericho chuckled. "Yes, I do."

"No, you like the image I'm creating around town. But you don't like me just for me."

He stared at her. "What are you talking about?"

"Let me put it to you this way. Do you think about me when you get up in the morning and wish you could be with me?"

His expression became so puzzled that Rayne didn't

have to wait for a verbal reply. She squeezed her eyes shut. The pain of embarrassment mixed with the pain of realizing that she didn't have the love of the one man she'd really, honestly, given her heart to and she almost couldn't say what she knew she had to say.

But she also knew she had to say it.

"You know what the funny part about this is? I think when my dad first left, when I was struggling with money, you really did like me. We were honest and straightforward and sometimes even argumentative." She drew a shuddering breath, shifting away, cool air pricking skin that had been warmed by his embrace. "I can't forget my past. I most certainly won't forget my dad. And I'm not going to turn into the perfect woman just because you decided that's what you want me to be."

Jericho shifted on the sofa, facing her, and caught her shoulders, forcing her to look at him. "You've got this all wrong."

She shrugged free. "No, you've got this all wrong. You want somebody who is perfect and that woman doesn't exist. I think I understand why. You don't want to be hurt. But what you don't understand is that we'd both be hurt more by committing to a relationship dishonestly." She drew a quick breath. "I think you better go."

Jericho nodded. "Yeah. I think you're right."

The next morning Jericho awakened in the bed in the room he was using in his parents' house and, oddly, his first thought of the day was of Rayne. Which was ironic considering she'd dumped him the night before because he couldn't say she was the first thing he thought of in the morning.

He rolled over to get out of bed, but stopped and squeezed his eyes shut. He *did* like her. He liked her a lot. He'd lusted after her for years. She'd grown into a beautiful, smart, savvy woman, somebody he could talk to, but she didn't think he was being honest with her—

Well, that wasn't precisely true. She thought he *had* been honest with her when her dad first left, but that he had stopped being honest because he didn't want a real relationship. Apparently, she was convinced he wanted a "fake" relationship. Whatever the hell that was.

The anger from that memory stoked his adrenaline enough that he did roll out of bed. He had no clue what she wanted, but he was glad that he hadn't slept with her the night before.

He frowned. Maybe he wouldn't go that far. But he was glad that he hadn't committed to her. She was a constant bundle of emotion. A determined, pushy, sexy, typically happy woman who seemed to like living her life in emotion-land and he was a normal guy who thought a life like that was chaos.

So she was right. They were better off not getting involved.

He showered, dressed in his police uniform and, in the kitchen, refused breakfast.

His mother groaned, "You can't skip breakfast."

"I'm already late. Besides, I like to get something at the diner."

"You're not late and I think that diner is part of your troubles," Elizabeth said, forcing him back to the table. "That place is full of gossips. A day away will do you some good. So grab a piece of toast and cup of coffee."

Ruthie's cry came through the baby monitor his

parents had sitting on the counter. Elizabeth undid her apron. "Rick's going to be here any minute to retrieve Ruthie so I'm going upstairs to dress her." She pointed at him, then the four pieces of toast and platter of scrambled eggs on the table. "You. Eat."

He sat, knowing that she was right—he not only had enough time to at least drink a cup of coffee and eat a piece or two of toast, but also a day away from the diner *would* do him good. Let Rayne wonder where he was for a change. He poured himself a mug of coffee from the carafe on the table and took two slices of toast. On a whim, he put eggs on his plate.

He had just picked up his fork when Rick walked in. "Where's Mom?"

"Getting Ruthie," Jericho said, spearing some eggs with his fork as Rick came to the table. "I'm a little surprised to see you today. I expected you to be on your way to your honeymoon."

"I am. I'm grabbing Ruthie and then we're off to the airport and the Bahamas."

Knowing Ashley's father had recently relocated to an island on the Bahamas, Jericho frowned. "You're spending your honeymoon with your baby and Ashley's dad?"

Rick laughed. "No. We got a hotel about twenty miles away from Ashley's dad. Gene and his fiancée want to spend some time with Ruthie, so they're taking her for a few days. Then we're all going to spend some time together."

"Sounds breathtaking and romantic."

Rick smiled and turned the chair across from Jericho so he could straddle it. "It's life. And I'm very lucky I found someone who accepts me, problems and all."

Rick's words reminded him of what Rayne had said about her dad. Rick's "problem" was a baby. A child he was honor-bound to raise. A child he *loved*. Rayne's "problem" was a dad who was trouble. Always had been. Always would be.

Though now that Jericho thought about it, no matter what Mark did, he was still Rayne's dad. And she did have a right to want him in her life. Jericho couldn't expect her to behave as if the guy didn't exist.

Jericho groaned. "Damn."

Rick grabbed a piece of toast. "What?"

"I think I might have made a huge mistake last night."

"What?"

"I think I insulted Rayne."

Rick smiled slowly. "Yeah. I saw you two together. What's up with that?"

"She's actually a very nice woman," Jericho said, jumping from his chair and grabbing his hat and jacket as he ran to the door. "And I like her a lot."

He didn't give Rick a chance to reply because now that he'd wasted time eating toast he might not have enough left to stop and see Rayne. Even though it was Sunday, she still went to work because the paper was due at the printer on Monday. Now that she had an employee, he couldn't really talk to her in the office anymore, so he had to catch her while she was still at home.

The drive to her house took about five minutes. It took another two minutes of knocking before she answered her door. Sleepy-eyed and with her hair tumbling around her sexily, she said, "Jericho?"

"I'm sorry."

"Sorry?"

"We had a disagreement last night, remember?"

She made a move to close the door. "We didn't have a disagreement. I realized that we have different kinds of feelings for each other. And it's not a good idea for us to see each other anymore."

He caught the door before she could close it. "I talked with Rick this morning and he told me he was lucky that Ashley loved his baby and things you said last night began to make sense. I was being short-sighted. I shouldn't have said that your dad was a problem. He's not a problem. He's your family. I get it."

Squinting as if she were trying to see him without her glasses, she shook her head. "I'm sorry, but I don't think you do get it. My dad's just a symptom of what's wrong with us. I love you. And you don't love me. You love an image. A woman with a clean slate, so to speak. No parents. No real past because with my dad gone and trying to turn the paper into something different I'm a fresh start." She took a long breath and her voice softened. "I think you like the blank slate, not me, and difficult as it is for me to refuse you, that's exactly what I'm going to do."

"Rayne—"

She shook her head. "Goodbye, Jericho."

She closed the door and Jericho fought the urge to pound on it until she opened it again and would listen to reason. But he knew her well enough to know that she wouldn't open the door again. She'd given him a real chance. Several chances, now that he thought about it. And he'd failed.

He'd lost her and the sudden, unexpected pain of that realization took his breath, but he forced himself to draw in air again. He swore he'd never let another woman hurt him and he wouldn't. He would survive.

Because that was what he did. He lost, picked himself up by his bootstraps and survived. This time would be no different.

So she was right. They really were over.

Chapter Eleven

Rayne spent that Sunday in tears. Though she knew she had done the right thing, she also knew she had thrown away her one chance. Jericho wouldn't approach her again. He'd told her he didn't want to be hurt and she'd hurt him. Probably not as much as she'd hurt herself, but she'd nonetheless hurt him. He wouldn't come back for a second helping. Still, in her heart she knew it was the right thing to do. She'd been in one relationship of convenience. It hadn't worked. She couldn't close her eyes and pretend this one would, simply because she so desperately wanted it. She had to be smart and step away and stay away.

Glad to go to work on Monday, she skipped going to the diner, afraid she would see Jericho. It would be difficult enough to go through the rest of her life knowing that she'd had a real chance with him, but she hadn't taken it. She could comfort herself with the knowledge that marriage to a man who didn't want her wouldn't work. No woman wanted to be married to a man who didn't want her. Every woman longed to be desired. And somewhere out there she was sure there was a man who would desire her and love her. But that didn't mean she had to see Jericho every damned morning. In fact, if possible, she wasn't going to see him at all.

That day she threw herself into explaining a new project she'd devised to increase advertising sales to Pete Forwalt. Tuesday she and Pete drove to Tucker where she introduced him to all the new contacts she had made for the place mat ads. Wednesday she let him go alone to the next town down the interstate.

Two days behind in her regular writing for the newspaper, she was so absorbed in the births, obituaries, anniversaries and social events that she skipped lunch. At two o'clock the rumble of her stomach reminded her that she needed food. Too hungry to hike home, she rose from her seat, slid into her peacoat and walked to the diner with her head down.

Passing the hardware, fewer than three steps away from the diner door and safety, she bumped into Jericho.

He caught her by the shoulders. "Whoa!"

She didn't even bother to look up. "Sorry," she mumbled, trying to shift out of his hold, but he held her fast.

"Rayne?"

She peeked up, catching his gaze, then wished she hadn't. She could see very real sadness in his eyes, and she darned near succumbed to it. But she couldn't. He wasn't in love with her. He was in love with the idea of settling down. She appealed to him because the townspeople were beginning to like her and she was really kicking butt at the paper now. So she was socially acceptable. She should punch him for being so cool and calculating about her when she was nothing but a bundle of emotion about him.

Instead she took a breath. "I'm okay."

Two or three seconds ticked off the clock before Jericho said, "Really? I slammed into you pretty hard."

"I'm fine," she said, still talking about their little run-in because it was a safe topic and she didn't want to venture into any of the unsafe things like how she felt about him. This close she could see the smoothness of his complexion, the stubble of his beard, the way the sunlight brightened his hair. She liked his voice. She loved his intensity. She needed someone with his integrity. But she also needed somebody who loved her, and he didn't.

"Look, I've got to go."

This time she succeeded in shrugging out of his hold and she raced into the diner before he could catch her. But being in the diner didn't stop the pounding of her heart, help to strengthen her breathing, or even make her feel slightly better. She loved him and he had absolutely no clue of how he affected her. If she didn't stay the heck away from him, one of these days she would either throw herself at him and tell him it was okay for her to settle for less than what she needed...

Or one of these days she would be walking down the street and that time when she ran into him, it wouldn't just be him. It would be him and another woman.

For a long time Jericho stared at the diner door, his heart in his throat. She'd told him she loved him, yet she could walk away. Three times. Part of him wanted to believe that she didn't understand what love was to be so flip about throwing it away. The other part knew that wasn't true. He saw real affection and emotion shining from her eyes when she looked at him. Nobody had ever looked at him the way she did. And he couldn't believe she would just throw all that away.

She'd said he didn't love her, but he did. He loved her enough that it hurt him more to see her pain than to endure his own. But she was strong and she was stubborn. She didn't believe him when he said he loved her and no argument he'd made changed her mind.

He'd lost her. And though it sounded foolish, he hurt more for her than he did for himself. But there wasn't a damned thing he could do.

Working late Saturday night, Rayne almost didn't hear the knock on her back door. At first the faint sound confused her, but when she finally identified it, she stopped working. There was only one person who knocked on her back door. Jericho. But now that she thought about it, even that was insulting. Right from the beginning he'd never entered through her front door, which was on Main Street, where people would see him.

She stormed to the back door, ready to be strong and tell him one final time that she didn't want any contact with him because every time she saw him it hurt. But as she navigated the boxes in her back room she suddenly realized that her real mistake was staying in Calhoun Corners. She could move up the road to Tucker and still do business exactly the way she was now. Pete could gather the information for articles for the *Chron-*

icle. All Rayne had to do was sell this stupid building. She'd tried to be brave but she could not go on living in the same town with Jericho and not be anything to him.

She angrily jerked open the door, but before she could open her mouth to say anything, Jericho grabbed her and kissed her. He kissed her hungrily, greedily and so sexily she melted in his arms, then he pulled away.

"I love you."

Dazed, she stared at him.

"I really, really love you, and before you tell me why I don't or how I can't, let me tell you that I found your dad."

She blinked. "You found my dad?"

"Yes, I needed to prove to you that I love you and I realized talk was cheap. I could tell you from here to tomorrow that I accepted your dad but it wouldn't mean anything. I knew the only way you would believe me would be if I proved it. So I did, by finding your dad."

"How did you find him?"

He grimaced. "I got the phone company records for your house from the night he called you."

"He didn't use a pay phone?"

"Nope. So I ran down the number of the incoming call and there he was, bigger than life, living in Omaha. We had a little chat and I brought him home."

"He's here?"

"At the diner. Ready to talk to you. Ready to work for you if you want him to. Or ready to leave again once the three of us spend some time getting to know each other."

Tears filled Rayne's eyes and she swallowed. "You do love me."

He nodded and enfolded her into his arms. "It appears I do."

"I love you, too."

He clung to her and, feeling his desperation, Rayne pulled back to look at him. "You weren't sure this would work."

He whispered, "No. I didn't know if I had pushed you so far I could never get you back."

She saw the hurt in his eyes and smiled at him. "You could never push me that far. I never stopped loving you. In fact, just tonight I decided the only way I could keep my sanity would be to move to Tucker so I didn't have to see you every day. It hurt that much to see you and know you didn't care about me."

"I do care about you."

"And I will never leave you. I will never hurt you. I will be the one person you can always depend on."

"And I'll be the person you can always depend on."

"Good because I'm not going through this courting stuff with anybody else."

"Me neither," he said, then he hugged her again. "I love you more than I've ever loved anybody else. If I had lost you, I never would have come back from it."

"Really?"

He smiled. "Really."

"So I'm pretty damned special, then?"

He laughed. "You're pretty damned special."

Looking into his eyes, Rayne knew that she was. At least to him. But that was all she really wanted. To be special to him. To make a life with him. Raise a family with him. Keep Calhoun Corners safe and quiet for their kids, their nieces and nephews, their parents, their friends.

"I guess we oughta go see my dad now."

"Yeah. Then I was thinking we'd give him your house."

Her eyebrows rose. "But he just gave it to me."

"I know, but I've been looking at one of the farms that's for sale on the outskirts of town."

"Oh, really?"

"My parents want to give us the down payment as a wedding gift and will lend us the rest—if you want."

"To live on a farm?"

"And earn a little extra money breeding horses."

She snuggled up against him. After having just saved a business, having somebody else find a home and another income was a genuine relief. "Sounds like a plan."

"Good, because it's a done deal. The farm is ours."

She gaped at him. "Really?"

"Yep, and the house is empty…except for a stove and a bed." He bumped his forehead to hers. "Wanna sleep with me tonight?"

She swallowed. "Yes."

"Good."

* * * * *

The next book in
THE BRIDES OF BELLA LUCIA
series is out next month!
Don't miss THE REBEL PRINCE by Raye Morgan
Here's an exclusive sneak preview
of Emma Valentine's story!

"OH, NO!"

The reaction slipped out before Emma Valentine could stop it, for there stood the very man she most wanted to avoid seeing again.

He didn't look any happier to see her.

"Well, come on, get on board," he said gruffly. "I won't bite." One eyebrow rose. "Though I might nibble a little," he added, mostly to amuse himself.

But she wasn't paying any attention to what he was saying. She was staring at him, taking in the royal blue uniform he was wearing, with gold braid and glistening badges decorating the sleeves, epaulettes and an upright collar. Ribbons and medals covered the breast of the short, fitted jacket. A gold-encrusted sabre hung at his side. And suddenly it was clear to her who this man really was.

She gulped wordlessly. Reaching out, he took her

elbow and pulled her aboard. The doors slid closed. And finally she found her tongue.

"You…you're the prince."

He nodded, barely glancing at her. "Yes. Of course."

She raised a hand and covered her mouth for a moment. "I should have known."

"Of course you should have. I don't know why you didn't." He punched the ground-floor button to get the elevator moving again, then turned to look down at her. "A relatively bright five-year-old child would have tumbled to the truth right away."

Her shock faded as her indignation at his tone asserted itself. He might be the prince, but he was still just as annoying as he had been earlier that day.

"A relatively bright five-year-old child without a bump on the head from a badly thrown water polo ball, maybe," she said defensively. She wasn't feeling woozy any longer and she wasn't about to let him bully her, no matter how royal he was. "I was unconscious half the time."

"And just clueless the other half, I guess," he said, looking bemused.

The arrogance of the man was really galling.

"I suppose you think your 'royalness' is so obvious it sort of shimmers around you for all to see?" she challenged. "Or better yet, oozes from your pores like…like sweat on a hot day?"

"Something like that," he acknowledged calmly. "Most people tumble to it pretty quickly. In fact, it's hard to hide even when I want to avoid dealing with it."

"Poor baby," she said, still resenting his manner. "I guess that works better with injured people who are half asleep." Looking at him, she felt a strange emotion she couldn't identify. It was as though she wanted to prove something to him, but she wasn't sure what. "And anyway, you know you did your best to fool me," she added.

His brows knit together as though he really didn't know what she was talking about. "I didn't do a thing."

"You told me your name was Monty."

"It is." He shrugged. "I have a lot of names. Some of them are too rude to be spoken to my face, I'm sure." He glanced at her sideways, his hand on the hilt of his sabre. "Perhaps you're contemplating one of those right now."

You bet I am.

That was what she would like to say. But it suddenly occurred to her that she was supposed to be working for this man. If she wanted to keep the job of coronation chef, maybe she'd better keep her opinions to herself. So she clamped her mouth shut, took a deep breath and looked away, trying hard to calm down.

The elevator ground to a halt and the doors slid open laboriously. She moved to step forward, hoping to make her escape, but his hand shot out again and caught her elbow.

"Wait a minute. *You're* a woman," he said, as though that thought had just presented itself to him.

"That's a rare ability for insight you have there, Your Highness," she snapped before she could stop herself. And then she winced. She was going to have to do better than that if she was going to keep this relationship on an even keel.

But he was ignoring her dig. Nodding, he stared at her with a speculative gleam in his golden eyes. "I've been looking for a woman, but you'll do."

She blanched, stiffening. "I'll do for what?"

He made a head gesture in a direction she knew was opposite of where she was going and his grip tightened on her elbow.

"Come with me," he said abruptly, making it an order.

She dug in her heels, thinking fast. She didn't much like orders. "Wait! I can't. I have to get to the kitchen."

"Not yet. I need you."

"You what?" Her breathless gasp of surprise was soft, but she knew he'd heard it.

"I need you," he said firmly. "Oh, don't look so shocked. I'm not planning to throw you into the hay and have my way with you. I need you for something a bit more mundane than that."

She felt color rushing into her cheeks and she silently begged it to stop. Here she was, formless and stodgy in her chef's whites. No makeup, no stiletto heels. Hardly the picture of the femmes fatales he was undoubtedly used to. The likelihood that he would have any carnal interest in her was remote at best. To have him think she was hysterically defending her virtue was humiliating.

"Well, what if I don't want to go with you?" she said in hopes of deflecting his attention from her blush.

"Too bad."

"What?"

Amusement sparkled in his eyes. He was certainly enjoying this. And that only made her more determined to resist him.

"I'm the prince, remember? And we're in the castle. My orders take precedence. It's that old pesky divine rights thing."

Her jaw jutted out. Despite her embarrassment, she couldn't let that pass.

"Over my free will? Never!"

Exasperation filled his face.

"Hey, call out the historians. Someone will write a book about you and your courageous principles." His eyes glittered sardonically. "But in the meantime, Emma Valentine, you're coming with me."

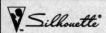
INTIMATE MOMENTS™

Don't miss the next exciting romantic-suspense
novel from *USA TODAY* bestselling author

**Risking his life was part of the job.
Risking his heart was another matter...**

Detective Sawyer Boone had better things to do
with his time than babysit the fiercely independent
daughter of the chief of detectives. But when
Janelle's world came crashing around her, Sawyer
found himself wanting to protect her heart, as well.

CAVANAUGH WATCH

Silhouette Intimate Moments #1431

When the law and passion
collide, this family learns
the ultimate truth—that
love takes no prisoners!

*Available September 2006
at your favorite retail outlet.*

Page-turning drama...

Exotic, glamorous locations...

Intense emotion and passionate seduction...

Sheikhs, princes and billionaire tycoons...

This summer, may we suggest:

**THE SHEIKH'S
DISOBEDIENT BRIDE**

by Jane Porter

On sale June.

**AT THE GREEK TYCOON'S
BIDDING**

by Cathy Williams

On sale July.

**THE ITALIAN MILLIONAIRE'S
VIRGIN WIFE**

On sale August.

With new titles to choose from every month,
discover a world of romance in our books written
by internationally bestselling authors.

It's the ultimate in quality romance!

Available wherever Harlequin books are sold.

www.eHarlequin.com

HPGEN06

SILHOUETTE *Romance* ®

COMING NEXT MONTH